The Church Of Irrelevance

A Novel by Mike T. Dark

Fuego Publications ♦ San Diego

This book is a work of fiction. The characters, incidents, and dialogue are drawn from the author's imagination and are not to be construed as real. Any resemblance to actual events or persons, living or dead, is entirely coincidental.

ISBN 978-0-9823494-0-3

The Church Of Irrelevance

Road Trip

1

I decided to write this story the moment I saw my church at the base of a towering column of smoke. As I ran up to the scene, fighting through the swarm of firefighters and onlookers, fighting the searing heat and choking smoke surrounding my face, while attempting to contain the shock, horror and fear battling in my mind, I knew it was my duty to tell the story. It's the story of my friend Sid, of the church he started, and indirectly, of me as well. Sid changed my life. His church changed the way I view the world. And even though the ravenous flames devoured everything, the church must live on.

To start this story, I have to go back, seven months prior to the fire, back to Lindbergh Field, back to The Day After:

"What's your issue?" said Nancy.

"Let's just stop in the bar first for a quick drink," said Sid.

"It's seven in the morning, Sid. Is it even open?"

"It's gotta be open; its happy hour somewhere."

"Can't we just get to the gate so we get a decent seat?" said Nancy. "We should be boarding in half an hour anyways--"

"Did you see that fog?"

"Yes, Sid. You spent all morning talking about the fog rolling through downtown last night. I am quite aware of the fog."

"The flight's delayed, I guarantee it. No reason to sit at the gate all morning."

"Don't you think you have had enough?" said Nancy, clearly losing patience with him.

"What is enough? Besides, I haven't had anything to drink since, like, one last night."

"Oh, really? Then where the hell were you until five this morning?"

"I already told you, just wandering around, thinking."

"Right, and the fog," she said sarcastically.

"Come on, one drink."

"Sid, I'm exhausted. I just want to get on the plane and go home. We have to work today don't forget. Monday, work, any of this ringing a bell?"

"Nancy, we can't go home."

"We can't? We have tickets, right?" she said in a panic.

"I can't go home, Nance. I just can't."

"Why? Because of work?"

"No, it's not that. I can't explain it to you. I can't even understand it myself, but I can't go home."

"What are we supposed to do then? Stay here?"

"Let's go to Vegas!"

"Sid…"

"I'm serious. You don't want to work today, and I'm not working today. Say it with me, Vegas baby!"

"We can't afford to go to Vegas, Sid. We couldn't even afford coming to San Diego. We're going home."

"Come on, humor me, just this once."

"Just this once? What do you think I'm doing here, Sid? I'm always humoring you, it's like my fucking full time job! What is your fucking problem?"

"Have a drink with me and let's talk about it."

"You are crazy!"

"Crazy is not a nice word, I think the more correct term would be mentally unbalanced."

"You're an asshole."

"Or you could go with an old standby, that works. I'm not going back today. I'm not ready."

"What does that mean?"

"I really don't know, honestly," he said with a look in his eyes she knew all too well. "I wandered all over downtown last night, just milling with all of the people, and something has changed. Something is different."

"All because of the game--"

"No, of course not. It's not that. I don't want to go back. I don't want to go back to work; I can't go back."

"What will a day in Vegas do?"

"I don't know."

"If you don't want to go back to work, just call in sick," she pleaded.

"It's not that easy."

"Why not?"

"I don't know! I feel lost. All of a sudden, I feel totally lost, and the only thing I know right now is going home is exactly the wrong thing to do. That life is over for me."

"What life? Our life?"

"No, of course not. You know I love you. I love that we flew out here on the spur of the moment, you made that possible. With you anything is possible," he said and took her hands in his.

"Except going home," she said and ripped her hands away.

"There is just no way I'm getting on that plane."

"That makes no sense."

"Probably not, but so what?"

"So nothing you do ever makes sense."

"Exactly!" he said.

"So go to Vegas."

"All right! Now you are talking," he said triumphantly.

"But I'm going home."

"What?"

"I'm sick of this shit, Sid. I'm going home. You do whatever you need to do, but I'm tired. I want to go home. I'm not following you on some wild goose chase again, I've had enough. Do whatever you want to do, but I'm going home."

"I need you."

"No, Sid, you need a shrink."

"Or a drink."

"Honestly, if it's not one thing with you it's another. Every single event in your life is blown out of proportion. Maybe you're lost, maybe you're mentally unbalanced, or maybe you're certifiable. But I'm not going this time."

"This is different, Nance," he said, his turn to plead.

"How's it different Sid? How's it different from flying to San Diego for a baseball game? How's it different from calling in sick because you wanted to stay up all night to see a sunrise? Or quitting your job because they wouldn't let you off on Groundhog Day?"

"That was a crappy job anyway."

"That's not the point; it's always something, and I'm not playing this time. You go play."

"Nancy--"

"No!"

"Look at me," he said.

"Why?" she said, looking at him as he requested.

"This is different. Please, believe me. I'm sorry I can't explain it, but I need you to be with me right now. My life's changing. I can feel it, and you are the only thing that can save me."

"Save you from what?"

"I don't know, myself maybe?"

"If you really want me to save you, then come home with me," she said, giving him one last chance.

"I can't! I'm sorry, I can't."

"Then I can't help you."

2

Nancy immediately went through security, down to Gate 26, and beyond that onto the plane sitting just outside the gate. Sid almost followed her, but, despite an overwhelming feeling that he would never see her again, the demons in his mind would not let him.

Did I say demons? Not literally demons, of course, and the associated imagery may be a bit over the top. Rather, the trio of internal forces that make up one's mind: emotion, logic, and intuition. Sure, the constant bickering and resulting internal strife may be the bane of many a person's existence, but no evil intentions drive their actions. A persistent pain, yes. But a demon? Most likely no.

"What is his issue?" you ask, as did Nancy. "Cut to the chase!" you demand.

I know, short attention spans just looking for the headlines, the blurbs, the sound bites. Any guesses out there? Does Sid have a secret? Not really. Did he sleep with someone besides Nancy? It's not that kind of story, I'm afraid. Sid killed somebody in the fog last night? Come on, definitely not that kind of story. By now you must be getting the hint that I am just teasing you and have no interest in telling you anything, at the risk of upsetting the rest of the story. But I must tell you something about Sid.

Sid is coming out of a closet. Not THE closet, but a similar experience in some respects. Sid has not been hiding something from everyone else, nor does he feel it's time to be more open with the world around him (sorry for the gross oversimplification). Sid has been hiding something from himself, and now the world around him is forcing him to be more open. The world is coming into his closet maybe the better analogy here.

I have three little voices in my head (honestly there are more in my case, but let's stick to the story and start with three), one each for emotion, logic, and intuition. Each one has a distinct point of view, a distinct opinion, and based on the collective consciousness--the combined affects of the three--decisions are made. For reason not yet realized, I believe Sid could only hear one force at a time, and, with more at stake than normal, the fighting between these forces was equally amplified.

Typically, as a person grows, he passes through various transitional phases that teach him how to be himself. First he learns there is a self. Next he learns how to relate with others. Then, he learns how to gain the acceptance of others--his family, his friends--by being the person they want him to be. Then, he must learn how to be himself, perhaps with the help of drugs and alcohol and other rebellious activities. And, finally, he learns how he fits into this world. Each stage is a rebellion against the former, an unlearning of what was learned in addition to new learning. This culminates with the balancing of the three voices in his mind, giving him the ability to be of one mind.

At some point in his cognitive development, I imagine Sid strayed from the normal path. I think he did not learn how to balance these distinct points of view. His system was built on the nature of perception and singular slices of an event that, when kept to himself, were unquestionably reliable. And it being singular singular with Sid, questions were extremely rare, as he had just one force guiding him instead of the many influences one would normally find. Who was going to ask any questions? Sure, sometimes it was Logic's voice, sometimes it was Emotion's, but it was never both. While that may seem simpler, the power struggle behind the scenes did have some unpleasant consequences.

As I see it, Logic had been on a power trip, sending Sid down the path he (I say he, I could say they, she or it, but who knows really? So, I say he) considered in everyone's best interest, but a mind cannot be controlled by Logic alone, just as it cannot be ruled by Emotion alone for a long period of time. If either side has too much control over perception or action, truths are hidden from the self and a war between Logic and Emotion. Intuition is a bystander for the most part. Logic believed it could win the war; Logic truly believed it was doing the right thing, but Logic cannot see what cannot be seen. Emotion disagreed with the path, but Logic had a stronger foothold in the mind due to the predisposition of the impressionable younger Sid. Emotion was forced into the background, getting a moment in the sun here and there (these few instances being the small aberrations mentioned by Nancy), but otherwise completely corralled up until this point.

Emotion had been planning a mutiny for quite some time, waiting patiently for exactly the right opportunity. Emotion knew that eventually the moment would arrive when something completely illogical would happen. When it did, Logic would be distracted by finding the perfect rationalization to avoid any confusion or ambiguity. Well, last night it happened. The world opened Sid's closet door. Logic behaved as expected, and Emotion pounced!

Free of the four-corner world run by Logic and in control at last, Emotion would not let Sid return to Phoenix and his regular, everyday life that Logic had created. Emotion and Intuition had decided a long time ago that issues needed to be addressed. Some truths needed to be revealed, understood, and accepted. Emotion had set a course for the land of no logic, Las Vegas. Las Vegas would help keep Logic at bay, fighting the many fights with Impulse, that wild child of Intuition, thereby leaving Emotion to chart the course. You see, taking over was just the first step in what could be a long journey of completing Sid. Peace and the return of homeostasis were needed.

Having been ruled by Logic for so long, Sid's approach to life had become very one-dimensional. All perceptions and actions were filtered through his squareness, and although this existence kept Sid even-keeled and almost happy most of the time, it did so at the expense of a very large part of himself. This path Logic had plotted was destined for disaster, yet despite all of Emotion's reasonable attempts to illuminate Logic, Logic could not see it coming and would not change course. That gets us to the point where Sid's problem takes center stage.

"What problem?" you ask. Patience. You will find out in due time. At this point in the story Sid does not yet understand his problems. It's only fair you find out together.

"Who am I?" you ask. Man, you ask a lot of questions. I'm Al. I'm the storyteller. I will tell you that I'm not some omnipresent narrator pretending to know the nuances and motivations of every single character in every single instance of this story. I try to read minds, I infer, I theorize for the sake of the story, I story tell, but alas, I am only human. I think it would be philosophically irresponsible in today's world, in this story in particular, if I didn't bring that up at the get go.

3

Yes, the airport bar was open. It was happy hour in London, and although it took Sid just a few beers to drown his self-doubt, it took him several hours to make his next move. The thought he would never see Nancy again scared him, and the nagging feeling that he would never return to Phoenix unsettled him even further. Not that he would miss Phoenix. All transplanted native San Diegans always assume they will make it back to live in San Diego someday. Phoenix was just a temporary station on that journey. Rather, his whole life suddenly seemed uncertain, rapidly changing from the logical flat square into what appeared to be an ever-expanding sphere of chaos! It was unnerving so he needed to nerve back up. A little liquid nerve recharge, courage 16 ounces at a time, was all he needed.

Unfortunately, and despite what you may hear, you can have too much liquid nerve. After a quick fight with the travel security agent, who wouldn't let him past security with a ticket for a plane that left an hour ago and another altercation with the ticket counter clerk, who repeatedly insisted all flights to Vegas that day were already booked, he decided he would drive to Vegas. After another hour wasted in lines at the car rental counter, and he was finally ready to go.

With the short night and waning beer buzz, it only took a little over an hour on the freeway for Sid to realize that he would not make it to Vegas without some help. He exited the freeway and found exactly what he was looking for: a man standing on the side of the road, next to the freeway on ramp, with his thumb up in the air.

"Where you headed?" Sid asked the man as he stopped and opened the passenger door.

"Vegas. You going that way?"

"Sure am. Your luck has already started!"

"Thanks, the name's Robert," he said after climbing in the car and reaching out his hand.

"Sid. Nice to meet you," said Sid with a sturdy, formal handshake.

"Nice car you got here, Sid."

"It's a rental."

"Yeah? You not from around here."

"Well, sort of. I grew up in San Diego, but I've been living in Phoenix for the last few years."

"San Diego. Now that's a nice place. I live in Anaheim myself, and I don't think I'll ever leave. What got you out in Phoenix? Work?"

"No, a girl."

"Ah, that'll do it."

"Yes it will."

"Are you going to Vegas for business or pleasure, Sid?"

"Maybe a little bit of both. How about you?"

"I'm going to see my son. A girl got him out of southern California as well. He lives out there with his wife and their brand new baby girl."

"Congratulations."

"Thank you. My first grandkid, I was beginning to think it wasn't going to happen."

"You don't say." Normally, Sid is not one for chitchat, but the circumstances being what they were and the small amount of liquid nerve still in his system allowed him to keep up for the most part.

"Do you hitchhike a lot?"

"Heavens no. Not anymore, anyways. My car broke down, I only made it 20 miles or so. Damn thing is practically brand new too. They just don't make Caddy's like they used to. I might have to get me one of those new Lincolns or something. Anyway, the car just died. The wife wanted to come pick me up, but I told here I would rent a car or something, but then I got to thinking that it ain't that far so I decided to hitch it."

"Not that far?"

"A few hours up the freeway, that's all. It used to be a pretty common thing. I hitchhiked all over the country back in my younger days."

"Really?"

"Sure. I reckon I've hitched this stretch a dozen times if not more."

"You know. I've never hitchhiked anywhere."

"I'm not surprised. It just isn't something you do nowadays. It was different back in the sixties. People were different. It wasn't a big deal at all. I never had one bit of trouble on the road."

"Reliving some of the glory days a bit?"

"Maybe something like that. Proving something to myself. Oh boy, if the wife knew about this, there'd be hell to pay!"

After a moment of silence he continued. "Like I said, my son just had a baby girl, Madison. The wife and I really didn't like the name at first, but it's growing on us. I haven't even met her yet, and she's going on six weeks old!"

"Why didn't your wife make the trip?"

"Oh, she was just out there for a few weeks actually. She has to get back to work. I was traveling on business. I'm retired mostly, but I still do some sales consulting work part time for some friends. I'd been a sales VP for, man, decades really so I have friends all over that throw some work my way from time to time. It has been a nice way to ease into retirement. It's hard to get used to not having goals and deadlines and whatnot. I also had to check on our property up in Tahoe. We are renting out our condo up there, and I hadn't been there in awhile. Anyway, I'd been here and there while she was out there, and I didn't want to wait until she was ready to go back. Also, my son has been really busy at his work. He represents some of the casinos in Vegas. He's a lawyer. He called me the other day and said things would be slow for a week so off I go."

"Wow, you're pretty busy for being retired."

"Keeping busy is my only goal in retirement."

"Why didn't you like the name?"

"Oh, I don't know. It was just foolish grandparent stuff, I guess. It just doesn't sound like a girl's name. Madison. It's a street or a city or something, and we were hoping he would name her after his grandmother, Dorothy, but they had their own ideas I guess."

"Kids will be kids, right?'

"Yes sir. He's doing really well for himself though. They have a nice house in a fantastic neighborhood. They both drive those big BMW SUVs. It's about time they settled down a bit too. He works a little too much, he needs to slow down."

"Yeah, you can't let work rule your life."

"So, what do you do for work Sid?"

"I used to be a network engineer for this company out in Phoenix."

"Used to be?"

"I'm pretty sure I lost that job. I still haven't called into work today."

"What in the heck are you doing out here then?"

"I'm going to Vegas."

"Why?"

"Because I want to and because I can. There is no 'why' really or I don't know why. Not sure which."

"You totally lost me."

"You were young once. You used to hitchhike all over the country. You know how it is."

"Maybe, but I was usually on my way from one job to another. I certainly wasn't renting cars to go from one place to another to avoid work."

"It's not like that."

"What were you doing in San Diego?"

"I went to the Padre games."

"Were you at that game last night?"

"Yeah."

"Boy that was some game--"

"Sir, sorry, but I really don't want to talk about it."

"Okay, suit yourself." Robert was taken back by Sid's abruptness on this subject. Things seemed to be going okay, but the look on Sid's face convinced him not to continue down that path.

"I'm sick of baseball anyway," said Sid, trying to be polite and change the subject a bit. "Such a scam. All winter we will hear the hype. Look at what we're doing to make our team better, blah blah blah. Every spring they get you all excited. Maybe this could be our year. Have faith. You are fed the hype and so desperate for any sort of hope, you gobble it up, hand over fist. All for a little hope. Such a pathetic lie."

"What?"

"Nothing, nevermind."

It was quite a few minutes before Robert started back up again. "So let's backtrack, you are in San Diego, supposed to go to work today."

"Seven o'clock this morning I was at the airport with my girlfriend, getting ready to fly home."

"What happened?"

"Nothing. I just couldn't go back."

"Why?"

"I'm not quite sure. I can't explain it."

"Are you kidding me?"

"Uh, unfortunately no."

"Where's your girlfriend?"

"She got on the plane. She went home. Actually, she's at work by now."

"Were you two fighting or something?"

"No, nothing like that. There's just something I have to do."

"So then you decided to drive to Vegas?"

"Yeah, basically. I wanted Nancy to come, but she wouldn't. She wasn't too happy with me, but I wasn't going back today. I wanted to fly, but there were no available flights and they kicked me out of the airport."

"What?"

"I was completely in the wrong, I can admit that."

"Boy, are you drunk?"

"No," Sid said immediately. "Well, not anymore. I don't think. Maybe a little."

"My word. So, for no reason, at least that you are aware of, you skip out on your girlfriend, skip your flight home, skip work, and decide you're driving to Vegas?"

"In a nut shell."

"Doesn't that sound a little crazy to you?"

"I don't know about crazy. Crazy is a pretty strong word. Maybe it was a bit impulsive."

"What did your girlfriend say?"

"She said I was crazy too. And an asshole."

"Whoo wee."

"Yeah."

"And I thought I was in trouble!"

"Yeah. I know it sounds weird, but ever since last night, something inside does not want to go back to Phoenix. Something inside wants me to go to Vegas, and this is maybe the first time I've ever listened to that little voice."

"You know, I have a son who is just like you."

"You have two sons?"

"Yes. Junior in Vegas and Christopher. He lives by the beach in this dumpy little studio apartment. He was a different job all the time. His car barely runs. He just loafs around the beach all day. He doesn't give a rat's ass about anything and changes gears at the drop of a hat."

"That's me?"

"You see, he's got no plan."

"No plan?"

"No direction. What are you going to do with your life?"

"I didn't realize I had to plan it all out."

"Of course you do. If you don't have a plan, you don't have direction, and if you don't have direction, you will never get anywhere."

"What if you don't want to go anywhere?"

"What?"

"Your son, Christopher was it? Is he happy?"

"Living in squalor?"

"Is he happy?"

"Like a pig in slop, just as happy as can be."

"So what's wrong with that?"

"He's doesn't have a house. He doesn't have a wife. He doesn't have a career. The boy has no future."

"So he would be better off with a career?"

"Uh-huh."

"A house and a wife?"

"Uh-huh."

"Even if he is unhappy?"

"That's not what I'm saying. I'm saying if he took some responsibility and had the house and career and wife and some kids, he could be happier."

"How do you know that?"

"That's what you do. That's life. Do you have any kids?"

"Hell no."

"Then, trust me. He would be happier."

"Basically he should have your life?"

"It's not my life. It's just the way things are done. It's the way God intended."

"Oh, brother."

"What now?"

"What 'God intended?' Isn't it funny how many different things we are told to do because it is what 'God intended?' It's just so ridiculous."

"It's the truth."

"What truth? What is truth? Your truth?"

"Just like Chris. I've been on this earth a lot longer than you son. I think I have a little better idea what I'm talking about. The world is not that complicated. You do what's right and everything works out."

"Jesus, you sound like some preacher."

"You say that like it's a bad thing."

"It is."

"Are you one of those atheists?"

"Maybe."

"What has God ever done to you?"

"It's not so much that. It's all of the people quoting God that I have a problem with."

"Why?"

"All the people that consider themselves religious, all it really means is they have this holier-than-thou attitude. 'I'm right. You are wrong. I'm chosen. You are a heathen.' It's all bullshit."

"You're generalizing. All church going people aren't like that."

"All people are like that. They go through their lives comparing themselves to everyone else and looking for any little thing they can use to put down others and inflate their own ego. Joe cheats on his wife; I don't cheat. I make more than Bob, that loser. Sure Jim makes more than I do, but he's an alcoholic. And church people do it more than most because they also have their religious beliefs to wield on the chopping block. Going to church doesn't make you any better than me."

"I never said it did."

"You didn't have to. I could hear the condescendence in your voice. Instead of measuring yourself against the standard of God or Christ, which you can't touch, you measure yourself against each other, against other religions. It's the new theory of relativity: I may not be good, but I'm better than you! It's such crap."

4

They went a ways in silence after that, each one stewing on the others' warped perception of the 'real' world. Sid had lost most of his liquid nerve so he didn't try to belabor his point. Robert, I'm sure, spent a good portion of the time questioning his decision to try hitchhiking again. The odds makers had moved the line on Robert ever hitchhiking again to 100-1.

"Get out of the way asshole!" Sid yelled at the car in front of him. "Look at this jackass, putting along in the fast line like they own the damn thing."

"They aren't doing anything wrong. Heck, they must be doing 75."

"He's totally locked me in. He's log jamming traffic! Look at all the cars behind us."

"They are going fast enough. You're the one speeding a bit recklessly, I might add."

"Fast enough? Who's he to decide what's fast enough? This is supposed to be a passing lane, not the I'm-going-fast-enough lane."

"Says who?"

"Isn't that a law? The left most lane should be used for passing?"

"I have no idea."

"It's certainly common sense."

"Common sense is to slow down."

"Now I have to get over. All the cars behind me have to get over just to get around the one clown who thinks he's going 'fast enough.' One car is all it takes to slow traffic. In a closed system like this, it just takes one person to ruin it for everyone."

"Oh, settle down. If you weren't going 90 miles an hour, it wouldn't even be an issue."

"One person can ruin everything. And why can't I go 90?"

"The speed limit is 65."

"70, but so what?"

"But what about safety?"

"So 65 is safer?"

"Hell, yeah!"

"What about the autobahn? Is that less safe than our highways because they go faster?"

"Of course."

"It's not actually. It's safer."

"That doesn't make sense."

"Oh it does! Think about it this way: people go as fast as feels safe, and if they don't feel like going as fast, THEY GET OUT OF THE FUCKING WAY!" Sid yelled at the car as he passed them on the right.

Then he continued, "That's logic. Logic makes it safer."

"You're just talking out of your ass. You don't know if it's any safer."

"Look it up. I assure you its true."

"But you're breaking the law."

"Oh, big deal. It's a stupid law anyway."

"It's still a law."

"So you agree that it's stupid?" Sid asked playfully before continuing. "I just have a higher risk tolerance."

"What?"

"I'm willing to accept a greater risk of getting a ticket by speeding. Those who do not speed are not willing to take any risk of getting a ticket. That's all. It's not that they're trying to be safer. It's not that at all."

"Just fear of retribution?"

"Right. Retribution. Good word. Using fear to keep people in line is as old as history itself."

"That's true."

"And did you further know that risk tolerance defines history."

"What?"

"It's true. Risk takers make history. The higher one's risk tolerance, the greater one's chance to make history. In any free society, low risk tolerance would be celebrated. Sure, we celebrate the risk takers in the business world, but only while they are on top, and we can't wait to knock them down. Everything else is clamped down by morality. Taking risks with drugs? Immoral. Sex? Immoral. Art? Immoral. Science? Immoral."

"Are you on drugs?"

"No. Are you?"

"No! That is about the dumbest thing I've ever heard."

"Well, I'm not on any illegal drugs. I may be a bit drunk still, but that's perfectly legal."

"Not when operating a motor vehicle!"

"Oh, well! Risk tolerance."

"You are one crazy son of a bitch!"

"Why?"

"Because you are."

"Because I don't subscribe to your truth?"

"Because you drive like a fucking madman and try to rationalize your way around it. Because you sit here spouting out this crazy shit and may actually believe it."

"I guess I'm only human."

"Now, what is that supposed to mean?"

"That's just what every single person on this planet does. Religion is all about the rationalization of your own sins while persecuting others because of theirs."

"Here we go again."

"Your truth, for example."

"My truth?"

"Yeah, you want Christopher to live life your way, not his way. Don't you get it? No one person should be allowed to dictate their beliefs onto others. No one person can decide what truth is just like no one can tell you what is fast enough. GET OUT OF MY WAY ASSHOLE!" Sid suddenly screamed at the driver in front of him while pounding his fist on the steering wheel.

"You can just let me out the next stop."

"Why? We're just starting to have some fun."

"I would like to make it to Vegas to see my granddaughter. I'm not sure you are intent on making it there alive."

"I know I'm poor driver. I just can't stand driving. I can't understand how someone can go poking along taking their sweet time going somewhere. When I'm driving, I want to get there now. There is no such thing as soon enough so I always drive like this."

"What, drunk?"

"No, fast. . . Drunk," repeated Sid with a giggle. "That was pretty funny."

"Barstow is coming up. There's a bus stop by the McDonalds off of Main Street. Would you let me off there?"

"Sure thing. You're much closer to Junior than Chris, aren't ya?"

"No! And that is none of your business!"

"You think I'm this raving lunatic, and yet I remind you of Chris."

"I was wrong. You are nothing like Chris."

"Why, because I'm a lunatic?"

"You said it, not me."

"You sat here talking up Junior and how great he is or, really, how much stuff he has. A car, a wife, a kid, a job, and then you only bring up Chris because he is some loser just like me."

"Chris is not a loser, you asshole."

"That's right. You said he's a loafer."

"Fuck you."

"I probably deserved that. Maybe I'm crazy. Maybe that explains the cold dark hole inside me all of a sudden. Maybe that explains the questions, the anger, the hatred of all of the lies, the sham of this meaningless existence that is driving me away from home, but then again, maybe not. You know what though?"

Robert was silent.

"Come on, don't clam up on me. The thing is that you don't know me."

"I don't want to know you. One hour with you is more than plenty."

"You can sit there and judge me all you want, but you don't know me. No one knows me. Hell, I don't even know me."

"What is that supposed to mean?"

"I have no idea. Crazy is such a strong word, I mean, how do you even know when you are crazy? What is your point of reference? Is it a slow climb down a long winding stairwell or is it a sharp fall off of a cliff? Ha, look at these symbols! Why is the assumption that it's a fall? Maybe crazy is a lifting of the spirit, an enlightenment, a freedom. Or, maybe all I want is a Pepsi."

5

After letting Robert off at the bus station, Sid decided that he needed another beer. Normally, his emotion was held in check, but since Emotion was driving today, he had run Robert a little ragged. Now Sid was ragged. This opening up and expressing his feelings stuff was new for him, and while part of it was fun, mostly it was so foreign it made him exhausted and real thirsty. He went straight to the nearest bar.

The nearest dive he could find was deep in the heart of Barstow. It held what was probably a typical crowd for an early Monday afternoon: a guy and a girl talking to the bartender at one end of the bar, a couple of guys by themselves at the other, a couple of empty pool tables. Sid sat at in the middle of the bar and before long had a pitcher.

"Hey, any ball games on today?"

"Dude, the World Series ended last night, the Pads--"

"Oh yeah, my bad."

The baseball season was over. There wouldn't be any more until February and spring training. Suddenly, a shiver ran up his spine as the world felt even colder than it had just seconds ago. Winter for Sid was the time of year when there was no baseball, and winter had officially started.

"They really need a baseball channel. What are we supposed to do all winter? Wait 'til next year? You get used to baseball being there for you. You rely on it, day in and day out. Then poof! It's gone! Just like everything else. It's like we're not even here, like we don't even matter. Like anything matters anyway."

"What?" said the bartender who hadn't been listening.

"Nothing. Nevermind."

In the olden days, I'm talking the early nineties here, you could judge the character of any bar by the jukebox. Jukeboxes used to house a fixed number of songs. Even the first CD jukeboxes had a finite number of songs, a lot more obviously, but definitely a finite number. That list was the list, no more and no less, and it determined the clientele which determined the atmosphere of the bar which gave the bar its unique character. The specific flavor of the songs gave that bar its own life. Fast forward to today and the dawn of the digital jukebox, many of which are connected to the internet so that if they don't have the song you want, for a little bit extra, it will go get it for you and there is no finite list. Any bar could be anything it wanted. As a result, bars became interchangeable, ordinary, and average, losing their life and becoming just a room with alcoholic drinks and customers. Now the clientele determined the atmosphere, and the bar has lost the ability to determine or even control that atmosphere. In fact, a single person could make any bar their bar, because if you want to play your song next, or play all of your songs next, for a little bit extra, you can be next. You can own the jukebox.

"What the hell do you think you are doing?" yelled the guy with the girl at the end of the bar.

"What are you talking about?" asked Sid, just returning to his seat from the jukebox.

"My song was next, what did you do to the jukebox? What the hell song is this?"

"This is 'Blasphemous Rumors' by Depeche Mode. I'm sorry about that pal; I didn't realize it would be a big deal. If you pay an extra quarter, your song will be played next."

"So you paid 50 cents for a song?"

"Actually, I had to download the song from the internet first. It wasn't on the jukebox, and that's 50 cents as well."

"You paid a buck for a song?"

"Actually, five bucks. I pulled down five songs."

"So my songs are after your songs now?"

"Yes, but you can play more songs and play them next if you want."

"I don't want to play more songs, I want to hear the songs I already picked, asshole!"

"Sorry, I didn't make the jukebox; I just played a song."

"Five songs."

"Well, yeah."

A couple of minutes later he was back.

"Are they saying what I think they are saying?"

"Probably."

"That's sacrilegious!"

"Sacrilegious to some, hilarious to others! Tomato, tomahto"

"How is that funny?"

"Come on, the thought that the whole world is some little toy just to amuse someone with a sick sense of humor is so poignant that you can't help but laugh."

"Jimmy can you skip this song. This is offensive," the annoying bar patron yelled to the bartender. "We are God-fearing people around here; we don't need your kind stirring up trouble or insulting us."

"My kind? What is that supposed to mean?"

"You can't just come in here and act like you own the place."

"They're just songs."

"Offensive!"

"Then you are really not going to like the next one."

"What the hell is this?"

"One of Us by Joan Osborne. Listen real closely."

"A slob?"

"Like one of us."

"That's it, Jimmy; kill this one too!"

"Come on."

"I don't like your attitude."

"I don't like your attitude either. They're just songs."

"Why don't you just leave us alone?"

"Why don't you leave me alone? And you owe me two bucks."

"I don't owe you shit; you played that crap."

"You can't hide from ideas."

"Enough out of you."

"There's still three more. Do you realize there are more stars in the visible universe than grains of sand on this planet! That God is a busy guy."

"That is not funny. Mister, I think you should leave," he said, now standing next to Sid.

"What? You own this place?"

"No, Jimmy's dad does, but he and I are friends. I know he has my back."

"Dude, I'm just a guy trying to have a beer. Why don't you just relax?"

"We don't like strangers around here. We always have people coming through town on their way to Vegas causing nothing but trouble."

"I'm not causing trouble. I just want a beer."

"Your songs are causing trouble."

"Then skip them."

"You are causing trouble."

"In a million years, the sun will die and take everyone with it, why can't we just get along?"

"That's not funny."

"I have a beer and I intend on finishing it."

"Finish your beer and then get outta here," he said as he returned to his seat.

"Whatever," said Sid.

He made his 'whatever' face to the guys at the other end of the bar to gauge if he had any support. From the glares he received back, he was pretty sure he did not. They skipped all of his songs, and though he was tempted to do it again just out of spite, he decided against it and just continued with his beer. He finished his glass and poured another when the fracas started anew.

"What the hell are you doing?"

"What?" a startled Sid asked.

"I said you can finish your beer."

"I'm not done yet, I have practically a whole pitcher left."

"That beer, I said that beer," said the guy now standing next to Sid, pointing at his glass.

"Too bad, when I finish that beer," said Sid with an over emphasized point at the pitcher, "I will go, okay? Jesus Christ!"

"That's it. I want you out of here now," he said as he grabbed Sid by the shoulders.

Sid stood up, shook him off, and turned around to face him. As he did, he noticed that Jimmy had come around the bar, and the two guys at the other end of the bar were standing up and coming towards him as well. Contrary to Robert's opinion, Sid was not suicidal.

"All right, all right, I'll go," said Sid as he started backing towards the front door.

"Good."

"This is so ridiculous. It was just a song, just ideas, absolutely nothing to get upset about. There is a great big world out there with lots of differing opinions on the truth."

"Shut up."

"You can close your mind, but you can't expect everyone else to close theirs as well. Are you going to kick my ass because of a song? Religious persecution does not have to be a way of life."

"I'm going to kick your ass because you are insulting me and my friends."

"Insults? You call those insults? If I insulted you and your brain dead friends, you'd know it. Those were just songs."

"Just shut the fuck up and get outta here."

"Isn't that exactly what the Jews said to Jesus before they had the Romans crucify him?" asked Sid, willing to leave but not without getting the last word. Unfortunately, that is the last thing he got out before the woman hit him in the back with a pool cue. As he dropped to his knees, he could see the others coming, and the blackness coming quickly after that.

6

It was the blinding brightness of a Barstow sunrise that finally woke him. Without any clouds to dampen its power and the red-tan landscape of rocks and sand, stretching all of the way to the horizon in every direction reflecting even more light, Sid got a sensation that the sun completely surrounded him. It was like waking up on the sun itself. It took three tries before his eyes could adjust and he could see where he was.

Sid quickly surveyed his current situation. He found his car on a hilltop facing east, staring directly into the blinding sun and overlooking the barren landscape. He checked his face in the mirror. There was some dried blood but no major damage and a lot of dried blood on his hands and his shirt. A bottle of tequila was resting comfortably in the passenger seat with about a quarter of its contents remaining.

It took Sid a few minutes to orientate himself, but it slowly came back to him. After being kicked around a bit, he finally crawled his way out of the bar and to his rental car. Bleeding from the nose and a cut above his eye, he made his way to the nearest liquor store and, after another argument, this time about his condition and lucidity, he purchased a bottle of tequila. The last thing he could remember was driving around town in his car with his bottle.

The anger from the previous day's incidents came rushing back almost as fast as the hangover headache. It was like a monster set of waves, and Sid was stuck inside the break. First the blinding sun, pow! Then the anger, pow! Followed immediately by the pain, pow! He couldn't take any more. He screamed at the top of his lungs as he stumbled out of the car, tequila in hand, pained by the stabbing in his brain behind his eyes. In a rage, he charged toward the apex of the hill and threw the tequila as hard as he could at the sun while screaming "Fuck you!" He watched it sail upward, gleaming brighter than the sun for a split second, in spite almost, before it crashed to the rocky hillside below and shattered.

"Fuck you! Fuck you! I don't believe! I won't believe!"

"What do you think you are doing? Do you have any idea what time it is?" said a woman's voice behind him.

Sid turned around and looked at her for a full minute, almost in disbelief.

"Grandma?" he said finally.

"Sid, is that you?"

"What are you doing here?"

"Well, Sid. I live here. The question is what are you doing here and why are you yelling at 7 o'clock in the morning?"

"I was, ah--"

"And where are your pants? And my goodness, what happened to your face?"

Sid looked down and indeed he had no pants on. He was also suddenly aware that he had no underwear on. His shirt didn't even hang low enough to hide this fact. He decided to skip that question and answer the easy one.

"I was jumped at this bar off of Main Street yesterday. I must have made my way up here before passing out."

"Goodness me. Let's get you inside and take a look at you."

7

Sid took a quick shower and changed his clothes. Grandma began attending to his wounds. There was nothing she could do for the bruised ribs and swollen nose so she focused on the cut above his eye.

"You're going to have quite a nice black eye here," she said.

"I figured that when I saw it in the mirror."

"Do you want to talk about it?"

"Not much to say, really. These guys took offense to the music I played at this bar--"

"Which bar?"

"The sports bar in the middle of town off of Main. They asked me to leave, and I was leaving since I was a little out numbered, but I tried to get the last word in--"

"Uh-huh."

"And this woman clocked me from behind with a pool cue."

"That explains the big bruise on your back."

"I went down and the others started kicking me before I could get out."

"It must have been some song."

"It's just a song."

"What was it about?"

"Well--" he said before pausing. This was not really something he wanted to get into with his Grandmother.

"You can tell me," she coaxed, sensing his reluctance.

"It was two songs actually, two songs that question the nature of God."

"Oh, really, how so?"

"One proposing that he is an idiot just like the rest of us and the other that he is one sadistic bastard."

"Aahh."

"I've been questioning the nature of things lately, and--"

"You find solace in people expressing the same angst."

"Yes, how did you know?"

"It's a very common thing, my dear. You're certainly not the first person to question your faith."

"Or lack there of."

"Sometimes just knowing other people feel the same way is a tremendous blessing. I think it is a main reason why the Church stays so strong. The community that develops between people becomes almost your crutch."

"Yeah?"

"You don't sound convinced?"

"Well--"

"Sid, I'm an old woman. I've been around the block, and there is nothing you could say that would surprise me. Tell me what is on your mind."

"The community feeling you talk about could also shut other people out."

"What do you mean?"

"A community is just a sub set of people. The minute you become part of one community, you close yourself off from others. You exclude other people the minute you define your community. Churches and religions can separate people. They're divisive more than connecting. They're an endless web of divisions and exclusions. I mean, I understand that religion came about because people needed a guiding force to answer the unanswerable questions and to link them together and build a greater good, but it just doesn't work."

"Really."

"They do bind people together, but only to manipulate them towards an end and pit them against another group of similarly bound people. These meaningless, almost arbitrary divisions create nothing but resentment, hatred, violence, and war. It's the bane of our existence."

"So, if there was no religion, there would be no hatred or war? Is that what you are saying?"

"Absolutely. Just look at history. War after war which are religious in nature."

"But you cannot just generalize that and extend it to all people and religions."

"Why not? The black and white nature of religion is what starts the process. You are Christian or you are not. You are good or you are evil. We are good; you are bad. We are right; you are wrong. All religious people see things this way, and every religious person that I've met has one thing in common: they are closed-minded. "

"I'm religious, am I close minded?"

"Of course not. You know what I mean."

"You mean outside the family, is that what you are saying?"

"Exactly."

"And how many people do you know outside the family that are religious? Do you ask people what their religious affiliations are when you met them?"

"Well, no."

"And are your friends religious?'

"No."

"Are you sure?"

"Well, honestly no. I know they don't make church on Sundays."

"Lots of people don't go to church but still believe in a religion."

"Maybe."

"What about Eastern religions?"

"Plenty of wars in the history of the east as well."

"I just don't see how religion could be bad."

"Because it causes you to judge people! Well, not you in particular, but, you know what I mean. You have your set of rules, and you judge people by the same set of rules even if they are following their own rules. You compare yourself to other people to satisfy your need for superiority. Everyone else is doing the same thing. It's such a sham."

"Seems to me that you could be doing exactly what you say they do. You're lumping people together in generalizations, creating absolutes, and judging beforehand."

"Maybe, but not to make myself feel better or glorify myself and my beliefs."

"Sure religions are a little backwards sometimes and maybe a bit behind the times, but they do not cause wars. People cause wars. People who lust after power or money or both cause wars. You see religion as the common denominator, but you are missing the most common denominator, people. There is good in all people, but there is also bad in all people, and there always has been. For every saint there are a hundred devils that have lost their way, lost the battle between good and evil, lost the line between right and wrong. If religion is used by some people as the basis for a war, you can't blame religion. It's still people carrying out the war. Blaming religion for war is like blaming the sheets for the shape of the bed."

"What?"

"It's what's underneath that counts."

"What is the whole point though? Do you really believe in heaven?"

"Of course I do. Why? Don't you?"

"It's just so perfect. It's exactly the kind of story you would tell a child. There's a paternal father figure watching over you, rewarding you with life everlasting if you are good. He is a God of love who just happens to have a ruthless streak. The dichotomy between the teachings of Jesus and God before him is sheer hypocrisy. It was when I got old enough to hear it told to other children, really hear the message with nothing but blind faith behind it, that I stopped believing. It was so long ago I stopped believing, and I just now realized it."

"But what is wrong with believing, even if it is just a fairy tale?"

"Everything. Believing one thing leaves the door closed for believing in anything else. Only one belief can be correct, and to admit someone else is correct would be to admit your belief is a fairy tale. There's no in between. It's one door or the other, and all of the closed doors are the problem with this world. This is a cruel, lonely world, and it's only made lonelier by religion. Sometimes…" his voice trailed off.

"Sometimes what, dear?"

"Ah nothing, forget it. I shouldn't have brought it up."

"What do you believe then? Reincarnation?"

"I don't know," he said in a whisper. "I didn't even realize I stopped believing."

"You have to believe something."

"You would think. I used to think…I used to believe…I don't know. Let's just forget it."

"Are you sure?"

"Yeah, forget it. I shouldn't be talking to you this way." said Sid, suddenly very self conscious of the fact that he was still drunk and once again expressing things he would rather not express, and to his grandmother, of all people. He wanted to run away and hide.

"Oh dear, don't worry about me. You aren't unsettling me. I'm worried about you, but our little talk won't shake my faith. I choose to believe. I'm not forced into believing. Everyday my faith affirms itself, and I'm thankful all over again. Life is a miracle; everyday is a miracle, and I thank my faith for it. Are you hungry dear?"

"Almost. Still a little nauseated."

"Some pancakes then?" she said and got up to start cooking.

"That would be great."

"So, where is Nancy?" said Grandma realizing that, for Sid's sake, the subject needed to be changed.

"Back in Phoenix."

"And how is she doing?"

"Pretty good," Sid started. "She is probably a bit pissed at me right now. We were in San Diego over the weekend, and we were supposed to fly back yesterday morning, but I couldn't get on the plane."

"Are you two fighting?"

"No, nothing like that."

"Don't you have to work?"

"Yes, but I couldn't go back," he paused again, but not for long realizing she would get it out of him eventually anyway. "It's really hard to explain. Did you ever have a feeling that if you went somewhere or did something, something bad would happen? You just feel so cold and empty all of the way to the core."

Grandma sat back down. "I have. One time."

"Are you okay, Grandma?"

"It was when you Grandfather died."

"Really? What happened? I thought he had a heart attack."

"Oh, he did. The day before, I had that feeling, so cold my bones ached. I was so worried that I begged him not to go to work that day. He told me that I was acting foolish, but bless his heart, he humored me and played hooky that day. We had lunch at Rosita's, and then he took me to a movie. That night he passed in his sleep."

"I'm sorry for bringing it up."

"Oh, pay no mind dear. We had a wonderful day and a wonderful life together. I have nothing but good memories. I'm fine, but I had forgotten about that feeling until just now."

"I'm sure that it's nothing like that, but that's why I didn't want to go back. Nancy called it a wild goose chase, and she is probably right," he tried to assure her.

"She probably is. That Nancy is a very smart girl, and we all like her very much. I hope you haven't messed everything up," she said as she got back up to continue cooking.

"Oh, I'm sure everything will be fine. It was a long weekend. She was exhausted and in no mood for another trip, but that reminds me, do you mind if I call her real quick? I haven't talked to her since."

"No, by all means. But do you mind a little advice?"

"Sure Grandma."

"Let her have her say, she will probably need to get some things off of her chest, and do tell her I said hi."

"Okay."

In about fifteen minutes Sid returned. Grandma had finished the pancakes and the table was set.

"Well, how did it go?" she asked.

"Well, she had something to say all right. I don't think I said three words!"

"I figured as much. She hasn't heard from you in a day and was probably a bit worried about you."

"I don't think she was worried."

"Of course she was. Did you tell her I said hi?"

"I did."

"And what did she say?"

"She said 'what the hell are you doing there?'"

"What did you tell her?"

"I told her I stopped here on the way because I was tired," said Sid. Another classic Grandmotherly look caused him to add, "Well it's practically true."

"Sid, you know darn well that is not true."

"I know, I know, but I don't want her to worry. Nancy is such a strong person, she's always there for me, and I've banked on that for so long, too long maybe. There's something I need to do. I'm not sure what exactly, but there's something I need to figure out, and maybe I have to do it alone this time. The last thing I need is to worry about her worrying. I already feel bad enough that I have you all worried, and don't give me that 'I'm fine' stuff; I can see it in your eyes."

"You have a look in your eyes as well, Sid. That's what has me worried. Your grandfather used to give me a look like that from time to time, and every time he was up to no good. That's what I'm worried about."

"Really?"

"Yes. I don't really know how to explain it, but I noticed it right away. There's a wildness in your eyes. You are on some wild goose chase, and don't shake your head; those are your own words!"

"Nancy's actually."

"So where exactly are you headed?"

"Vegas."

"All by yourself?"

"Yeah, just real quick."

"What are you going to do there? Where will you stay?"

"I will probably just go to the Luxor and see if they have any rooms available. I don't really know what I'm going to do. I haven't thought that far ahead."

"Why then? Why not just stay in San Diego?"

"I'm not sure. I have to."

She was silent; Sid was ashamed that he was worrying her so. He did not like sharing or burdening them other people with his worries.

"Thanks for breakfast Grandma. It was great, just like I remembered."

"You're welcome dear."

"Do you mind if I lay down for a bit for a quick nap. I'm pretty tired."

"By all means, dear. You can use the spare room up front. The bed's already made."

"Thanks Grandma."

8

It was almost dark before Sid finally woke up. When he did, he finally understood his plight. He finally found the source of his turmoil. Even though he had long ago abandoned his religious upbringing, he had never out and out denounced it, not even to family, not even consciously. But somewhere along the line he had buried it a long time ago and hid it from himself. He couldn't deal with the fact that life had no meaning or that existence was pointless. He couldn't cope with the emptiness of space and time, couldn't escape the torment of self, and couldn't face a worthless future. He couldn't face a life with no God, no afterlife, no reincarnation, no nice happy ending fairy tale and just an end. It had been buried deep, but it was buried no longer. This was what he believed, and he had always believed it, actually. Now he had to face it and accept it.

The big questions made him feel small and cold. They were an almighty belittling power. He could no longer deny that this is the way he felt. He could at least accept that. He just didn't know how to go on. He didn't know how to function without the faith and hope that underlie everyone's action. No matter what religion a person has or does not have, they have a foundation of beliefs based on hope that they build themselves upon. They have a meaning behind their actions, a meaning behind getting up everyday. It may change over time, but it does not change over night. He had been lying to himself for years, and now he found himself with nothing. Sid now had no hope, no meaning, no direction, no foundation, and no reason to get up in the morning. Without that, how could he go on?

He made the bed as best as he could and then found Grandma in the living room doing a crossword puzzle.

"That was quite the nap."

"Yeah. I guess the last few days finally caught up with me. What time is it?"

"Almost five. Are you hungry? We could go to Rosita's, my treat."

"Thanks Grandma, but I should hit the road."

"You're leaving tonight?"

"Yeah, I should."

"Wouldn't you rather go tomorrow? You're more than welcome to stay."

"No, I had better get going."

"You sure?"

"Yes, thank you though."

"Okay, suit yourself. Can I pack you a snack for the road?"

"No Grandma. Really, you have done quite enough already. Thank you for breakfast and the talk. It really did help, and don't worry about me. I will be fine." He gave her a hug, then picked up his bag and readied to leave.

"I've been thinking about what you said, Sid," she said, stopping him for the moment. "Sometimes what makes this world seems so alone is when you try to make a go of it on your own. We all love you very much, and I'm sure Nancy does too, no matter what she said."

"I'm sure. I've never doubted that at all."

"She is a good person. You can trust her with your feelings as well."

"At some point, I will. I promise."

"People like to demean being together, calling each other the ball and chain, being tied down and what not, but it's not so much 'tied down' as a tether. It lets you be yourself but keeps you grounded, you keep each other grounded, and you always have someone by your side to fight through times like these. Nancy is a fighter."

"I know."

"Together you are stronger. Together you can get through anything."

"Thanks, Grandma. Thanks for everything. I love you," he said with a goodbye hug.

"I love you too. It was great to see you again."

"And don't tell Mom and Dad about this. I don't want to worry them as well."

"Okay, dear. That goes against my better judgment, but I won't tell them. I promise."

"Thanks. I will see you again soon. Don't worry about me, I'm fine."

"Bye bye dear."

Sid couldn't even look his Grandmother in the eye when he left, and he could not get out of there fast enough. He wanted to stay for Grandma's sake and to ease the worry written all over her face, but had to get out of there. He needed to be alone and he needed time to think. He made a quick stop at a liquor store before heading out on the road again.

His mind was a whirlwind of thought. Much of the trip made sense now. The reason he had to go to Vegas was clear to him. Deep down, he knew Nancy wouldn't come, and that was no accident. He couldn't stay in San Diego with so many family and friends around just like he couldn't stay at Grandma's. He didn't have time to be polite and engaging. He had crap to figure out. He wanted to be alone because he felt alone. He had to be alone because he alone had to deal with this, and he had to deal with it because he was paralyzed by it. The lie was over, something had to takes its place, but what?

Living without religion is easy. As long as you are not faced with anything to test your resolve, the question of religion barely comes up on a day-to-day basis. It's also easy to knock religion. The desperation inherent in belief is both comical and sad. You can denounce religion, but how can you denounce people? Denounce humanity? His Grandmother surprised Sid. The thought that people were the lowest common denominator had never occurred to him. Certainly this changed things, but how?

As he thought himself in circles, he continued on his way, driving through the deep darkness of the nighttime desert towards Las Vegas. With the radio off, the only sound he could hear was the car on the road, the occasional crack of a beer can being opened, and the whirling dervish of a fight in his head between Logic and Emotion.

Las Vegas

9

Logic and Emotion were in a full-fledged fistfight. At first, Emotion just enjoyed being at the helm and interacting with the world after being pent up for so long. Expressing his feelings and the playful dialogue with Robert was exhilarating. Telling off the bar folk was equally as fun, at least until the beating started, then not as fun.

Emotion believed they were at least on the right path, but Logic thought Sid was completely out of control. Logic felt Emotion had gone too far and now he was pissed. Logic had worked for years to prevent this very day of reckoning, and Emotion ruined everything Logic had worked towards! The lie? Exposed! The plan? Lost! Sid's life? In shatters! Logic taunted Emotion with the results of the last two days: Nancy, gone and not returning! Sid battered and beaten! Now Grandma? Did Emotion have no shame?

Emotion fired back that the delay in dealing with this problem was the cause of the tremendous upheaval experienced lately. That was Logic's fault, not Emotion's. If Logic hadn't buried this so long ago, none of this would have ever happened in the first place! If Logic had listened to one single thing said by Emotion for all of these long years, this could have been avoided. But no!

Logic believed their very survival was at stake now and wanted no more talk of this weak and whinny drivel. There was no time for a philosophical discussion on the meaning of existence. He had to get Sid under control, and if he had to use violence, then violence it was. Logic threw the first punch.

The fighting raged for hours. Impulse set the odds at 3-2, Logic, while Intuition took the underdog. Neither side would give in.

Neither side accepted any blame. Neither side had the faintest idea what the other was talking about, but each side was exhausted. Arms were tired from throwing fists and blocking fists. Bodies were tired from repeated blows. Minds were tired of the endless loop of what each considered the same drivel repeated ad nauseam. Mouths were tired of repeating said nauseam.

Impulse lost interest in the fight the moment Sid reached the Nevada border. The bright, blinking lights greatly outshone this meaningless fight in his opinion. The battle was slowed by the ever-increasing buzz that they were all feeling as Sid drove through Nevada. Logic and Emotion under the influence, is this possible? Of course! No one escapes intoxication, no one! The battle was at a virtual standstill when they saw the light that lets you know you have reached Las Vegas shooting out the top of the Luxor to the stars, one of the few man made structure you can see from space. At night, you see it well before you reach the city, the tease that is Vegas. Then you climb one last hill and descend on the brightest city ever built, Sin City, the Mecca of decadence, Las Vegas! When you see all of the lights below you, anything seems possible. The world is beautiful and grand. The past is lost and the future is neon! Distracted by that glimmer of hope, Emotion let down his defenses and was cold cocked by Logic, who swiftly assumed control of the subconscious.

10

Sid woke to the sound of a phone ringing. It took him four rings to realize it was the room phone in his suite and another two to answer it.

"Hello?" he said feebly.

"Sid?"

"Nancy?"

"You sound horrible."

"I'm okay. How are you? It's great to hear your voice. Wait, how did you find me?"

"Grandma and Zeke called yesterday. She's very worried about you."

"I know. I feel terrible about that."

"She said you would be there and that I should come and get you."

"I knew she was worried, but I'm okay, there's nothing to worry about. You don't need to come out here."

"Too late for that. I'm here."

"Where?"

"In the hotel lobby. What room are you in?"

"You are?

"Yes."

"That's great! I'm in room 2901. Come on up."

"Okay."

"Wait! Are you there?"

"Yeah, I'm still here?"

"You have to have a key to get to my floor. I will come down and get you."

"Okay, I'm at the phones by registration."

"I'll be right there."

In minutes, Sid brought Nancy back up to the room. It was a plush room near the top of the Luxor Pyramid with a large living and dining room, a private bed room, full bar, and an expansive window overlooking the strip. Nancy was appalled.

"How are you paying for this?"

"Don't worry about it. It's taken care of. Pretty nice, huh? Check out how far you can see. I tried to stay up until the sun rose but I didn't quite make it."

"I see," noticing a trash can full of empty beer cans. "What's going on, Sid? Can you tell me? You've sure got Grandma worked up."

"It's very hard to explain."

"Please try. Does it have to do with the other night?"

"Maybe. I don't know if it was that night or not or if it was just a long time coming. I've spent a lifetime denying things and leaving things unresolved and burying my head in the sand basically."

"Like what?"

"Big picture stuff," he said, but after one look into Nancy's concerned eyes, he knew he'd better start at the beginning. "I walked out of the last bar that night in a pretty good mood still at the time, and the city was covered in this fog, but all of the lights from the city and the ballpark made the fog glow. It looked almost supernatural. I was literally dumbstruck for a moment. I even stopped walking I think. I thought to myself, 'It's the big Padre in the sky smiling down on us.' I distinctly remember that, and all of a sudden it hit me like somebody telling me 'you don't believe in God, stupid.' Then the wonder was gone, and I realized that I really don't. Before long, I realized I have no faith or hope whatsoever. Everything that I thought I believed in was a complete sham of emptiness."

"What? How?" Even she was at a loss for words. "How does that happen?"

"It's very hard to explain. I barely understand it myself."

"But just like that?"

"Just like that! And then I didn't know what to do."

"But you had to go to Vegas?"

"I had to go somewhere where I could be alone and think."

"Vegas?"

"Sometimes very crowded places are the loneliest of all."

"But you invited me?"

"I know, and here you are."

"I just don't understand how all of a sudden--"

"You know, I don't even know if you believe in God or not?"

"You know I'm not religious."

"That's not what I'm asking. At the end of the day, do you believe there is a supernatural power out there and some meaning to your existence?"

"Well, of course, doesn't everyone? Don't you?"

"No, not at all."

"Since when?"

"For a very, very long time now."

"Really? I had no idea."

"See, neither did I. I never faced it. I buried it. I hid these thoughts from myself."

"How? Why?"

"I don't know. Its cliché, but the mind does work in mysterious ways. It scares me."

"It scares me too!"

"It does explain why I've stumbled my way through this life recklessly. Basically, deep down I must have understood there's no truth to my stupid existence."

"Don't say that."

"Don't say what?"

"That you aren't here for a reason."

"Why?"

"Because you are."

"Maybe I'm not."

"You are!"

"You see, that's what I'm talking about, that conviction. That's faith! I have no faith or conviction. I'm lost. I used to mock people's conviction. Now I'm jealous of it. It's very peculiar to be without it."

"You're really freaking me out!"

"I'm sorry."

"Now I know why Grandma was all freaked out."

"I know. That's why I wanted to be alone."

"But you shouldn't be alone, not like this."

"This is my problem. I have to figure this out."

"Not alone," was all she could muster out before sitting down on the bed. To say she was shocked would have been an understatement. Knowing how impulsive Sid could be, she was afraid that he may start down a path and not be able to stop, but she was also afraid of Sid. What kind of person talks this way?

"What if there is no God? What would you do?"

"You mean like rob a bank or something?"

"Just imagine that there's no meaning to your life, what would you do?"

"I would kill myself," she said suddenly and started to cry.

"I know," said Sid, wrapping his arms around her. "I'm sorry. This isn't fair."

"Are you…did you try to kill yourself?"

"Why would you say that?"

"From what your Grandmother said and your face and all the beer and those bottles on the bar."

"I may have had way too much to drink in Barstow. I'm not quite sure, but no, I'm not planning on killing myself."

"Why not?"

"What?"

"I don't know. I don't know why I said that, but there has to be something keeping you here, right?"

"You would think so, and I've been hell bent on destruction these last couple of days, but I realized as I drove into town last night that death is not an alternative."

"Why not?"

"Because if heaven is true, what a crappy and crowded place that has got to be! You know how I hate crowds. If even a fraction of the 100 billion or so people in history ever made it to heaven, what a nightmare!"

"Not funny."

"Oh, come on. If reincarnation is true then I would have to do this all over again. Either case isn't exactly a solution."

"And you don't believe in either anyways," she said and almost cracked a smile.

"Right."

"What if there really is nothing?"

"One can only hope."

"What is that supposed to mean?"

"Nothing, sorry. I'm so sorry, this is my problem, not yours. I'll get through this, don't worry."

"Don't talk like that anymore, okay?"

"All right, all right. It's okay."

"You seem so different. It's like I don't even know you."

"Sure you do. Sure you do. It's the same old Sid. You'll see."

"I hope so."

"Do you think you understand, you know, my issues?"

"I think so. It's scary and sad. I can see why you've freaked out."

"I have, haven't I?"

"Not that I could blame you."

"I never meant to scare you or freak Grandma out. I just didn't know what to do. I still don't know what to do."

"You should call Grandma."

"That's a good idea, if I let her know you are here, she will be reassured."

11

Sid woke up well before Nancy but continued to lie in bed watching her sleep. Grandma had been right. Opening up to Nancy had made a world of difference. She may not have completely understood, but as the day wore on she seemed to forget about it. The awkwardness and fear born out of their initial talk had dissipated by breakfast. The rest of the day had rolled out like nothing had ever happened; they ate out a few times; they tooled around Vegas doing the couple things that couples do. Maybe she just accepted it and accepted him and wanted to help him through it. Things seemed normal by the end of the day and that was all that mattered to Sid. Having Nancy there with him and for him, soothed him like nothing else would have. Their bond seemed stronger than ever before, and it inspired him. Quietly, he got up and went into the other room to watch the sunrise from the expansive view from his window.

As he sat there, he stared out across the desert at the sun rising over the hills, illuminating the sleeping city, slowly filling the dark shadows. As the city was gently bathed in sunlight, his new path illuminated before him in synchronicity. A peace settled over Sid and he was all too aware of it. He was positive it had everything to do with Nancy. Suddenly filled with a sense of purpose, he quietly went to the desk and pulled out the yellow pages. After finding what he was looking for, he wrote her a quick note, put the yellow pages away, and headed out the door.

When he came back in the door two hours later, Nancy was awake, dressed, and eating the breakfast that she had ordered from room service just like he'd requested.

"Good morning!"

"Where have you been? What are you up to?" she said with a smile.

"I stood right here this morning watching the sunrise and suddenly everything was so clear to me. I can't even explain to you how much better I feel today, and it's all because you are here. You make me complete. You fill up the dark spaces in my heart; you are my sun."

With that, he got down on one knee in front of her and took her hand. Oh yeah, he was wearing a tuxedo.

"Nancy, will you marry me?"

"What are you talking about?"

"Let's get married here, today. There are a hundred chapels; we can get you a ring and a dress and--"

"Sid, be serious."

"I've never been so serious in my life. Your being here is like a miracle."

"It's not a miracle, Sid."

"It is! It is to me. You saved me."

"Sid."

"I'm serious."

"I'm sorry, Sid, but I'm not marrying you."

"All right, not today then. We can plan something then so our families can be there, but let's do it. Let's take the leap."

"No, you did not hear me. I don't want to marry you, not today, not ever."

"What?"

"Sid, I'm so sorry. I didn't want to have to do this today. I'm glad you were able to get a lot of things off your chest. I'm very glad you feel better and I really thought I understood, but it took me a long time to fall asleep last night. I kept going over and over it in my head, and as much as I love you, you're a mess."

"But that's all behind us."

"How can you be sure? You've always been a mess."

"It will be different, I promise. Look at me. I'm sure."

"I'm not. I mean, you have this crisis on what I would have thought was the best day of your life. You eat, drink, and sleep Padre baseball. They finally win the World Series, the World Series Sid! And you are there, at the game!"

"I know."

"And then what do you do? You drop off the deep end! That makes no sense! I thought I knew you, but I don't and--" she stopped, suddenly afraid of going to far.

"And what?"

"Just take a look at things from my point of view. You're a day removed from a probable suicide attempt, you quit your job again, you put yourself up in a room you cannot possibly afford, and suddenly you want me to marry you?"

"I told you that the room's all taken care of."

"What does that even mean? You don't take care of anything, Sid! You bounce from job to job. You're unreliable and reckless. You're a complete mess. I can't marry you." She paused for a second. Sid was sitting in a chair by the window obviously in a state of shock.

"Listen, I love you. You are a great guy and a lot of fun, but I don't want to save you. I didn't come here to save you. I don't want to be your crutch. At some point, I need someone to take care of me, but you are not a provider. I don't want to live in our apartment forever. At some point you have to get serious and start making some money."

"Now, it's money. Money is so worthless."

"It is to you, but not to everybody else. I want a nicer place, a house even. I want a nice car and nice clothes. I want to live in a nice neighborhood and have kids someday. I want a better lifestyle, and I don't see you providing that, not now, not ever anymore."

"Things will get better from now on. Trust me."

"That's just it. I don't trust you. I thought I understood. Really, I did, but, after I thought about it last night, I kept wishing you had never said anything. You scared me."

"How many times can I say I'm sorry? And since when do you want kids?"

"Since always."

"I never knew that."

"We had never talked about it, but you know I love kids."

"Yeah, other people's kids, not ours. I would never bring a kid into this worthless world!"

"How can you say that?"

"Easy."

"You don't mean that."

"You know what I imagine when I picture myself with a child? I imagine the day when they are fourteen or so and they are just starting to get it or when they are nineteen when they are really getting it, and they come up to ask me, 'why did you bring me into this shitty existence?' That thought sends shivers up my spine. There is no greater birth control than that. Never."

"That's horrible."

"Whatever. It's not like it matters anymore."

"You know, not everyone contemplates existence and whatnot. Some people, many people in fact, are happy believing what they believe."

"Fucking lemmings."

"Screw you! Look in the mirror pal! It was just a baseball game!"

"Just a game? It was my fucking holy grail!"

"And you won! You got it! What's the issue?!"

"I was never supposed to! Don't you get it?! It was supposed to be unattainable. It was supposed to be there for me forever. It was my faith. It was my hope. It was always there just out of arms length, just far enough away for me to keep reaching for it, but close enough to stay in perspective. Then it happened, and I had it in my hand, and my hope was gone. Meaningless, just a game."

"It never had any meaning. It was always just a game."

"It's just a game, now. Sure, before it was like fucking heaven. Then I went to heaven; I got to see my nirvana. And you know what I found? I found out that it was just another fucking Circle K in Yuma, Arizona, and there's one on every other fucking corner."

"Nice," and with that, she got up and started packing her stuff.

"It's true. Dreams are dreams for a reason. Realizing a dream just drags it into reality and mucks it all up in the process."

"I'm sorry to have to do this to you today, but my flight is schedule to leave in a few hours and I think it's best if I go."

"Whatever."

"Are you going to be okay?"

"Peachy."

"You aren't going to do anything reckless, are you?"

"What do you care? Why don't you just go marry some fucking lawyer or something!"

"I still care, asshole! I do love you! This is hard on me too!"

She began to cry as she continued packing. Sid just sat in the chair watching her.

"You're right. I'm sorry. You should go. I will be fine."

"You're such an asshole."

"I know."

"I just have to go."

"I know. It's fine. You should go."

"Are you sure?"

"Yeah, I'm sure. You should go."

Sid swiveled in his chair and stared out the window as she packed. The sun continued to rise ever so slowly farther and farther away from the mountains.

12

Logic was devastated!

Since the night Sid had lost his hope, Logic knew what Sid needed most was to bury hope into something else. With his vast vulnerability, any remotely plausible philosophical pinnacle would have seemed like the golden life raft of hope. Logic buried hope in baseball all of those years ago, and, for nearly two decades, Logic, Emotion, and Intuition peacefully coexisted, but don't think that that wasn't tough to pull off! Sure, Logic was calculating and merciless in planning the death of Sid's religion, but with the important role it plays in any psyche, Logic had to be equally calculating in creating Sid's new religion. And sure, it's easy to rationalize baseball's similarity to religion, but rational thought gets you nowhere when talking to Emotion and Intuition! Emotion and Intuition don't care about rationality. They depend upon religion to control fears that arise from the unknown. It was impossible to convince them just to live with their fears. Fear is a genetically engrained reaction to stimuli designed to protect you, but these base genetic responses have little or no place in today's world. There are no predators tracking our every move, nor danger around every corner.

In order to keep Emotion and Intuition appeased so long ago, Logic had to appeal to them in individual and subjective ways. Baseball was already entrenched in the psyche of a young Sid through years of little league, backyard baseball with his brothers, baseball on the radio and on television every Saturday as a youth. It was already part of his culture, all Logic did was emphasize certain things and embellish others just a tad.

Emotion had always been in awe of baseball for many different reasons ranging from the dynamic of the pitcher/batter duel to the sometimes painful highs and lows that were an opiate for Emotion. The community of likeminded fans certainly helped create a nurturing environment where everyone supports, consoles, and protects one another. A grand, majestic 'church' was filled 81 times a year in cities across the country and all followed similar rituals that were, in many cases, a hundred years old. Going to that church was a transcendent experience that seemed like the first time every time. The senses are inundated by their surroundings including the cacophony of sounds, the din of the crowd with its ebb and flow along with the drama, the PA announcer and the organ music, the magnificence of the stadium towering and enclosing the greenest of green grass ball field with its lights, signs, a scoreboard, and, finally, a game. Going to games held Emotion in amazement and Logic used this ploy every time he felt faith falter in Emotion.

Baseball even has The Book, the unwritten rules that dictate the code of right and wrong. When tweaked slightly, The Book has been applied successfully in any given situation. Nearly everything necessary was already in place before Logic set his plan into motion. Logic emphasized the uniqueness of being a major league player and how rare it is to make even the minor leagues, then how just a small fraction of those ever make the Bigs. In no time at all, Logic had Emotion convinced that these are not mere mortals he was watching. They were supernatural beings. Baseball Gods. And all you have to do is watch them day in and day out, that thought is reinforced on a daily basis. As Ted Williams used to say, 'hitting a round ball with a round bat is the hardest thing to do in the sports world.'

With Intuition, a different path was required. Intuition has a long standing fear protocol. Its fear of fears and subsequent fear stratification drives almost all their opinions. Intuition required a grander understanding of the Big Picture, which could then be used to determine the appropriate fear protocol and keep Intuition functioning normally. As previously mentioned, that Big Picture was a championship for our beloved Padres. Each day, the current standings are published to let you know exactly where you stood in relation to the Big Picture. In addition, Intuition also loved the play by play guessing game. Each baseball game involves hundreds of tactical decisions between the batter and the pitcher or manager and manager that can be second guessed. In every case, the feedback is immediate and almost always drew an according response from Emotion, which is fun in its own right.

Each quickly adopted the new religion so long ago, and the success of this plan, compared to the disaster of the previous two days, convinced Logic all he needed this time was a quick, semi-permanent patch job of Sid's psyche. After regaining control from Emotion, this patch job had been the priority. Nancy showing up on the doorstep to rescue him was like a gift come straight from God, or the fates, or karma or that cosmic chick flick writer in the sky. The plan scripted itself requiring just a gentle push "Marry your savior and you shall find salvation," Logic said. And did you see that sunrise? Logic's timing was flawless! Sid bought it. Of course he bought it. It was the first constructive thought in a few very long, mostly sleepless days. Logic was so confident that he bet Impulse they would be married before sunset and even gave Impulse odds of 10-1. Order and sanity were so close Logic could taste it, and together they tasted like milk chocolate!

The patch job was working right up until Nancy killed it! How could this be? Who is in charge of that subconscious over there? And kids? Where in procreation did that come from? Where was Logic supposed to hide the boogers and shit, worry and pain? How could Logic keep Sid light and breezy under the tremendous responsibility of parenthood? Once that subject was broached, Logic realized control was impossible. No patch job could withstand it. Even a pseudo crisis such as this would eventually present itself and this would start all over again. At that moment, Logic gave up, went to the corner and cried himself into a deep exhausted sleep.

Surprisingly, Emotion took the news even harder! Even though he disagreed with yet another of Logic's short term solutions which would assuredly continue to deny them their regular voice in all matters, Emotion loved love! It was a high like no other. Any plan involving love immediately was approved by Emotion. Hell, it was a romantic plan too, and Emotion is such a sap when it comes to stuff like that. Wedding bells, white dresses, doves carrying ribbons, eternal happiness was all that Emotion saw. Then Nancy violently stabbed the love to death with her doubt, fear, and rejection. Beset by bitterness, Emotion immediately took sick and was bed ridden.

Tending tenderly to both was Intuition. Of course, Intuition expected this would happen, but Intuition was not responsible for things as they happen, only before and after. Intuition never helps make a decision and accepts no responsibility for a decision. It only offers hints of choices and glimpses of consequences, real or imagined. But while Intuition may have expected Nancy's decision, he was not expecting the collapse of both Logic and Emotion. Such an event was unprecedented!

Who then was in control? You guessed it: Intuition's wild child Impulse now had control of the ship. Impulse quietly waited for Nancy to leave, allowed Sid to help her with her bag and into a cab. After Sid watched the cab disappear into traffic, Impulse said ever so gently, "You need a drink."

13

Sid walked back into the hotel and slid up to the first bar he could find. He calmly sat down, patiently waited first to order and then to receive his drink. You would never have known he was in the midst of a Luxor sized personal crisis. To the man seated next to him, he seemed like an ordinary guy, who happened to be in a tuxedo. That man sitting next to him would have, in fact, bet good money that this was going to be a good day for Sid. That man sitting next to him was just happy to see someone else at the bar this morning. Mostly, that man sitting next to him was just looking for a little conversation. The man sitting next to him was me

"Just charge it to the room please, 2901." said Sid to the bartender.

"Would that be the honeymoon suite?" I asked.

"What?" he said, startled, like he didn't even know I was there which he probably didn't.

"Trying to calm a few pre-wedding jitters?"

"Oh, the tux. I was hoping to, but, unfortunately, I'm not," he said as he turned to me and gave me a weak smile.

"Ooh shit. Did she hit you too?" I said when I noticed his black eye.

"Oh, that? No. That was. . . yesterday?" he asked himself. "The day before that?"

"Hey man. I'm sorry. I had no idea."

"Not your fault, just the way things happen I guess. Sid," he said as he extended his hand.

"Al. What happened? She leave you at the altar?"

"No, never made it that far. I had this crazy idea that we should get married. It was a pipe dream really. I was marrying the idea, not the person. The odds of it working were long anyway. It's probably for the best."

"So you proposed?" I asked.

"An hour ago, yeah."

"And she said no? Wow. Where is she now?"

"At the airport. It's pretty much over. As I watched her pack just now, I ran through the conversation to see where I went wrong, but it's nothing that happened today. I know that. Like many things lately, this is one of those things that was a long time coming, but even though I understand that, looking at her and watching her and even thinking of her right now, even though they are good thoughts, happy thoughts, it's still hard to face."

A spontaneous moment of silence erupted which I had to end so I said "All ends are hard to face. Let me buy you a drink."

"Oh no. I'm okay."

"No, I insist. I'm traveling. I'm just going to expense it anyway."

"You can do that?" said Sid.

"Sure, who's going to tell me I can't?"

"You're here on business then?"

"Yeah, my company's annual sales convention. Well, my old company actually. I'm in the process of handing things off. I'm just here to shake hands and reassure people. After two days of it, I didn't feel like sitting through another day so I'm laying low. Hopefully I'm free for a couple of days. I'm not heading home until Friday."

"So where's home?" he said.

"San Diego, how about you?" I replied.

"No kidding! San Diego! Me too!"

"Really? Imagine that."

"Actually, I've been living in Phoenix for awhile, but I plan on moving back," he said.

"Oh yeah? When?"

"Probably tomorrow. Maybe the next day."

"Shit, did she kick you out too?" I asked.

"No, nothing like that. I never liked Phoenix and really never wanted to go back. Now I have no reason to."

"That's seems like quite a story. You okay?"

"Other than being completely in limbo, I'm…not really sure what I am," said Sid. He sat and looked at his drink pensively for a few moments. "Did you know there are more stars in the sky than grains of sand on the planet?"

"No, I've never heard that."

"How does that make you feel?"

"Thirsty. Sir, two more over here. Put them on my tab," I said.

For the rest of the morning and into early afternoon, he told me the story you have been reading. Yes, it is true, much of the story I've told here is as I heard it from Sid himself, and that is an inherently flawed recollection. But rest assured, I've done some due diligence: I conferred with Grandma, who talked to Nancy a couple of times in the soon to be ensuing months, as well as a couple of other characters who have not yet joined the story and shall remain nameless. I've tried to keep the story as impartial as possible and put forth my best effort at a little bit of bullshit farming, but the bottom line is that every story is just one person's point of view. Isn't history even, nothing more than just someone's opinion of events that have taken place? The very minute something happens on this planet, at least four different recounts take place, such is the nature of perception. Besides, you are well aware even a single person can see things two ways. After all, just ask Emotion and Logic. You cannot separate yourself from an event any more than you can separate fat from bacon, nor similarly would you want to. Truth is just hturt spelled backwards and means as much, nothing more, nothing less, so deal with it.

By the time I was caught up to the present, we were having dinner in one of the restaurants in the hotel. I was having a lot of trouble with parts of the story.

"Let me get this straight: you went to game seven?" I asked.

"Yep."

"Greatest game ever!"

"Absolutely," he said with a huge grin.

"And it destroys your life."

"So far."

"That makes no sense. I like baseball as much as the next guy, but come on! You have to be kidding yourself," I said.

"Not at all. It was just as crushing as if my Mom had died."

"Knock on wood," I said.

"Of course," said Sid, already knocking as I spoke.

"Still."

"I've thought a lot about this over the last couple of days, and it still makes sense to me," he said.

"Honestly?"

"Think of it this way: all religions are created to answer the unanswerable questions. Why are we here? What is the meaning of our lives? What happens when we die? Blah blah blah. None of these questions have verifiable answers, and that uncertainty troubles our finite minds. So you are left with half answers relying on belief. You cannot know the answers to these questions, but you can believe you know the answer to these questions. Okay so far?"

"Okay," I conceded though with some trepidation.

"That belief is faith. Faith fosters hope. Hope is the essence of any philosophy or any religion. I pretty much avoided much of that conversation and found my hope in baseball. Yeah, I know. That's stupid, but a benevolent father figure watching all six billion people every minute of everyday is not stupid?"

"Good point."

"So stupid comes with the territory. And baseball has a lot of the same qualities as a normal religion. Each fall, most teams die, one team is immortalized, but most teams die. My team always died which is an important part. Each spring, each team is reborn. There is always a hope for tomorrow. Each spring hope itself is renewed. Each day, no matter what happened yesterday, no matter who you are playing or how the team has faired all season, there is hope. Any given day your team can win. It is a constant in your life. It is a rock, a foundation. It is there everyday for most of the year. It has been there as far back as everyone you know remembers. It has history. It has a language all its own. It is a more perfect world--a world of symmetry and order, a world unto itself that is simple and segregated from the rest of life's problems. It is something that joins people together and gives them a frame of reference for individuals to relate to a larger group, and it is a good religion. It is a religion built on failure rather than the guilt of not meeting perfection. The best pitcher still gives up two or three runs a game! The best hitter is still out over 60% of the time! The best team loses 60 games a year. Failure is expected, and it is dealt with on a daily basis. It gives you a dream and a goal, a championship, for which to strive: to win the World Series. That was my religion. That was my holy grail. Well, we did that, and what I expected it to be the end-all of end-all feelings. I expected glory and some sort of transcendent peace, and I got nothing. Nada. Zip. I expected fulfillment, and I still have nothing. I made it to heaven, and I'm disappointed. I reached nirvana, and it is ordinary. How do you recover from that?"

"I don't know," I said.

"One part doesn't make sense. One fallacy I found in my façade is why didn't I see that winning wouldn't be everything I thought it would be? Baseball teaches you to deal with failure. The lows don't get low, and the flip side is that the highs don't get high. I should have seen that coming."

"Whoever thought it would happen though?"

"Exactly!" he said.

"The odds of them winning it all were like--"

"120-1. I know."

We paused to reflect on that for a second before Sid started it up again.

"What do you believe? Do you mind if I ask? Do you believe in God?"

"No, I don't mind. I don't believe in God actually, but it's something I'm comfortable with for the most part."

"Let me ask you this then, do you have a wife or kids?"

"Yes, both," I said.

"Imagine they were just killed in a car crash, where do they go?"

"Shit man!" I said, almost choking on my beer.

"Sorry."

"You're bumming me out here."

"You don't think about these things?" he asked.

"I try not to. It would be the worst thing imaginable if something were to happen to my boys. I try to avoid thinking about it."

"It's what I've been thinking about for days now, and I can't stop the thoughts. The thoughts that I never considered now scream at me, demanding an answer, which I don't have, and leave just that cold feeling in here," he said pointing to his chest.

"Jesus."

"Nancy said that she wished I would have never shared this with her. I think she's right. Part of me wishes the Pads had never won it all."

"Nonsense. You may be down right now, but it will get better. You will figure it out."

"How?"

"I have no idea. Let me call my wife real quickly. You've got me all freaked out. Then, we will figure out how to break your funk."

14

When I walked outside to find a quiet place to call my wife to make sure she was still alive, I saw a sign for karaoke at a different bar in the hotel. I've always been a bit of a music nut, so I thought this was the perfect way to forget a little pain and have some fun. When I got back, Sid was not impressed.

"Are you kidding?" Sid asked.

"No, not at all."

"I hate karaoke," he said

"Have you ever done it?" I asked.

"I told myself I would never sing karaoke."

"Why?"

"Not quite sure right now, but it sounds like a bad idea," he said with a laugh.

"I do it all of the time; it's a blast."

"Really? What songs do you sing?"

"Lots of things."

"Oh, good. I was afraid you had like one song that you're good at and sing it every time."

"Oh, yeah. I have that too. Every time I'm at a new place I sing the same song," I said.

"Oh, great! You're one of those people! What song is it?"

"'Every Breath You Take' by the Police."

"Not a bad song," Sid said.

"And I nail it. Come on. It will be fun. What else are you going to do? Get married?"

"Man, that's a low blow."

"Sorry," I laughed. "So sorry, but I've wanted to say that all day."

"I should change."

"Hell no! You're dressed perfectly for a little karaoke."

"I know. That's what I'm afraid of!"

It seemed pretty late to us, but there were only a few other groups in the bar and just a few singers ahead of us. I grabbed a couple of song books while Sid picked up the drinks.

"Look at these people. What do they all have in common?" I asked.

"Delusions of grandeur?"

"Absolutely. This is hope personified; look at them living a dream one bar at a time. This should be right up your ally!"

"Is that supposed to be uplifting?" he asked.

"Kinda. . . missed?"

"Yes," he said.

"Find your song."

"I'm not doing it."

"You are, and you will like it," I demanded.

"I'm not."

"Come on. There has to be one song that you wouldn't mind singing. At least look through the book."

"I will look, but I'm not going up there."

"Sure. Whatever. I'll be right back; I want to get my name in and see how long we have to wait to sing."

"I can't believe they have it," said Sid after I returned from my performance.

"What?"

"'Dear God' by XTC. You know that one?"

"Sure. You could do that; that's pretty easy, right?"

"It's pretty short. I wouldn't think it'd be too hard."

"Do it!"

"Naw. I can't." His enthusiasm was gone as quickly as it had sprouted.

"Sure you can! It's exhilarating!"

"It's so lame," he said.

"Sure, it's lame; sure, it smacks of desperation, but you lose yourself. I promise you a big time rush, and it comes from doing something outside of yourself. For three minutes you are a completely different person. Live in the moment; forget the past; forget the future; focus on right now. People paralyze themselves because they are either focused forward or backwards. Live in the now! This moment! Everything that has happened these last three days has driven you, in a tuxedo, to a karaoke bar! This is your moment."

"That was better."

"You think? Not too over the top?" I asked.

"No, a subtle mix of motivation and philosophy. It was quite nice actually."

"Are you going to do it?'

"Sure," he said although he still sounded reluctant.

"Great, I will put your name in!" I filled out the form and ran it up before he could change his mind. I still believed a little distraction was all he needed. Although I was supposed to be next (yes, again), I asked them to let Sid go before he lost his nerve.

When the song started, Sid was unsure of himself and quite awkward, but after the first "I can't believe in you" at the end of the first stanza, he started to get into it. I had assumed he was getting into the singing and performing, but he seemed increasingly lost in the words. Looking back, I figure the song expressed something he had been feeling for days now. Animosity toward Robert, the bar in Barstow, religion, Nancy, and his current plight poured out into his voice when he killed the second stanza. He was carrying the microphone and stand, belting through the chorus, all with his tux still on! I was a little jealous. He looked sharp up there. It wasn't bad singing for his first time either.

The first sign of trouble came when the host grabbed at the end of the microphone stand in an attempt to get Sid to put it back on the stage. It was a subtle hint that Sid wasn't allowed to carry it around, but Sid yanked it away and held it parallel to the ground out of the guy's reach. The host seemed intent on shutting Sid down and climbed up on the stage. He only took one step toward

Sid before Sid pushed him back off the stage as he sang "I don't believe in," just before the big crescendo ending. No one heard a word after "I won't believe in," because Sid started swinging the microphone stand like a baseball bat at the equipment on stage. Sparks flew everywhere as I watched him sing the final forty seconds with a conviction that froze me in my tracks. I never even tried to stop him. As he destroyed the entire stage before being wrestled to the ground by security, it never even occurred to me that he should be stopped.

He was completely calm as he was marched out of the bar in handcuffs. He even smiled at me as he went past; he then yelled back to me, "Just have them put the damage on the tab and charge it to my hotel bill. I'm good for it. Tell them I'm good for it!"

Maybe I pushed to hard. Maybe karaoke isn't for everyone. Maybe we were a little too drunk. Maybe I should have been worried when he chose 'Dear God' by XTC. Considering his current state of mind, maybe I should have known that Impulse was the one driving the ship and they had always wanted to smash up a karaoke machine. I felt responsible for the whole mess, and I vowed to do what I could to get him out of it.

15

Despite my best efforts, Sid stayed that night in jail before being released to me the next morning. I picked him up in his tux and black eye, but not looking any worse for the wear.

"Are you okay?" I said after we left the building to look for a cab.

"Oh, I'm fine. I got some sleep. No big deal."

"So, I got the hotel to drop the charges if you pay for all of the equipment."

"Great. You know what? I never thanked you. You have been such a tremendous help, sticking by a complete stranger," said Sid.

"Do you need any help with the bill?"

"Naw, I'm okay."

"Are you sure? I feel partly responsible here."

"Man, that sun is killing me," he said, shielding his eyes and looking up at the clear blue sky.

"The total is over five grand, do you--"

"I got it; don't worry. This is not your fault, you know. I don't blame you in any way. I made this mess for myself."

"It probably wasn't the best idea I ever had."

"It was a great idea. You were trying to help, you laid yourself on the line and really tried to help. That is still amazing to me."

"I was just sucked into the moment, I guess, sucked into the story."

"Five grand, huh?"

"Yeah."

"Does that sound a little high?"

"Actually, I thought it was a little low. They must have been able to salvage some of the equipment. That stuff is expensive."

"I guess it was worth it then."

"What?"

"It was worth the five grand. Man, did that feel good!"

"I know I won't ever forget it."

"Yeah," said Sid, "but now what?"

Sid sat silent and somber on the way back to the hotel. With all of the tasks associated with cleaning up the mess and getting him out of jail, I had temporarily forgotten about his troubled soul. I wished I had some words of wisdom, some magic to share, a soliloquy on the grandness of being and the importance of every human life, but I was beat, just as Sid was, and my idea coffer was empty, so we sat in silence on the way to the hotel. It wasn't until we walked into the hotel that someone spoke, and that person was a stranger to me.

"Sid!" said one of two men rushing towards us. "Where have you been?"

"Jail."

"Shut up!" said the other as they all exchanged hugs.

"I'm serious. Al just bailed me out," he said motioning to me. "Al, I'd like you to meet my brothers, Jerry and Zeke. Guys, this is my friend Al."

"What did you do now?" asked Zeke. "You're face is worse than I imagined."

"It's a long story. What are you guys doing here?"

"Well, Grandma called me to get Nancy's number on Tuesday, but she was cryptic about the whole thing. She kept saying that she couldn't tell me." Zeke continued, "Then Nancy called Grandma back yesterday when she got home, unfortunately, before she called me. Then Grandma called Mom--"

"Oh, no!"

"Oh, yes, so Mom called Jerry, Jerry called me, and we decided to get up here as fast as we could and made it in last night. Of course, you were nowhere to be found."

"And Mom has left like a dozen messages," added Jerry.

"Oh shit!"

"Yeah," said Jerry.

"Well, we better go call her," said Sid.

"Why don't you give me a call later, Sid," I said. "Let me know how things go. I'm in room 419."

"Why? You have someplace to be?"

"No, but--"

"This will just take a second. We will just run up to my room and make a few calls. I can get out of this monkey suit; then I think we should hit up that champagne brunch."

"Are you sure? Your brothers are here--"

"Nonsense. Besides, you don't think I'm going to tell them this story on my own, do you?"

16

After Sid got off the phone with his Mom and Grandmother, he jumped in the shower. While Sid washed away the previous day, Jerry and Zeke had some questions for me.

"So, do you live out in Phoenix?" asked Zeke.

"No, I live in San Diego," I answered. "Are you guys living in Phoenix?"

"No, San Diego. Do you know Sid from college or something?"

"No, I just met him yesterday."

"Really?" Zeke seemed taken aback by this.

"Yeah."

"And you bailed him out of jail?" asked Zeke.

"Technically, I didn't have to bail him out. As long as he pays for the equipment, the charges will be dropped."

"Equipment? How much?" asked Zeke.

"Five grand."

"Holy shit," said Jerry.

"What in the heck happened last night?" asked Zeke.

"Sid sort of demolished the karaoke set up at the bar."

"What?"

"How?"

"With the microphone stand," I said as I swung an imaginary bat to demonstrate.

"Holy shit!" exclaimed Jerry. "Sid sings karaoke?"

"No, that was my brilliant idea."

"What's going on with him?" asked Zeke.

"You know, I don't know," I only had part of an idea and it didn't seem my place to tell. "He was really quiet this morning when I picked him up. That could have been because he is sober now, feeling a little ashamed, not really in any condition to open up to essentially a perfect stranger."

"Let me cut to the chase, Al," said Jerry. "Grandma and Nancy think he is a danger to himself. What do you think?"

"Jer, he barely knows Sid. Why--"

"Zeke, I'm just asking a question. Will you let the man answer?"

"No," I said quickly. "I don't think he'll do anything rash."

"Anything else, you mean. He destroyed a bar last night!" said Zeke.

"It was just the karaoke machine," Sid and I said in unison as he emerged from the bathroom.

"You guys been talking about me, eh?" Sid asked.

"Just a little bit," answered Jerry. "We are just trying to figure out what is going on with you."

"How far did you get?" he asked.

"Not far," said Jerry.

"We know you got beat up in Barstow, we know you were in jail last night, we know Nancy came and went in a hurry, we know everyone is worried about you. That's about it," said Zeke.

"We didn't really get into anything while you were in there," I said.

"Then we have a lot to catch up on. Who's hungry?"

Over breakfast, Sid ran through the who's, what's and where's of his last four days. From a high level though, certainly not the philosophical version he gave me the day before. I gleaned a few items from the conversation: Sid was notorious in the family for doing wild stuff, reckless and irresponsible going way back. Jerry was amused by his antics, Zeke acted as if the devil himself had possessed his brother. And apparently, Nancy was viewed as something close to a saint for not only putting up with him, but for calming him down, for the most part, during the time they had been together.

"You actually proposed?" laughed Jerry.

"What in the world were you thinking?" exclaimed Zeke. "No wonder she took off. You totally blew it!"

"It seemed like a good idea at the time. I was just flailing, completely lost, but she was right. It wasn't going to work. I will not be able to live my life on the straight and narrow with the house in the suburbs, kids, steady job, dog and cat. Man that is not me. Once I accepted that's what she was looking for, it made understanding her leaving much easier. It would have happened eventually. I just pushed the issue."

"Why is that life a bad thing?" asked Zeke.

"For him, Zeke," said Jerry.

"Nothing's wrong with it, I just can't do it. I'm in no way judging that life, it's just not me."

"Sometimes I think that is exactly what you need, it will calm you down!"

"Zeke, not everyone needs to be you."

"Screw you, Jer! I'm not the only one that thinks it!"

"You're right; Mom is going to be pissed!" laughed Jerry again.

"She already is," said Sid with a laugh. "She laid into me pretty good on the phone. She told me to get my act together, go back, and beg Nance's forgiveness!"

"Did she really?" I asked.

"Oh yeah. My mother and grandmother have loved Nancy from the first day I brought her to a family function. Master's degree, great job, very out going, sensible, smart. They would ask each other, 'what's she doing with him?'"

"They did not," said Zeke.

"Yeah, they did, actually," said Jerry. "Who told you that?"

"Grandma actually asked Nancy that very question."

"Shut up!" said Jerry.

"It's true," said Sid.

"What did she say?" asked Jerry.

"I can't remember, some crap. Nance was just stunned. She blurted out some stuff about how nice I was or something. I don't even remember," said Sid with a laugh.

"What did she see in you?" asked Zeke.

"Zeke!" said Jerry before bursting out in laughter.

"I'm just asking."

"It's a valid question. Something must have kept her around for these last couple of years. Maybe she saw something that wasn't really there. Maybe she thought I would change or that she could change me. Maybe I offered her some freedom in an otherwise controlled life. Maybe she liked the way I made her laugh all the time. Maybe she just felt obligated to keep me around since I moved out there for her. Who knows?"

"Maybe she was using you to get to Zeke," said Jerry, starting another round of laughter.

After the laughing subsided, Sid looked really serious all of a sudden.

"What is it?" I asked.

"Oh, nothing," he said and tried to feign a smile, but Sid is awful at hiding his feelings, he looked like someone walked over his grave.

"Seriously, what is it?" asked Jerry.

"Nothing, just one of those moments when you remember that it's over; that part of my life is over. Nancy is gone, done. It's nothing, but the finality, the emptiness, just catches me off guard a bit."

"What happened next?" said Jerry, trying to change the subject.

"This is where Al enters the story. I put Nancy in a cab and went straight to that bar over there for a drink. Al was sitting there, ditching work, I might add, and he thinks this is the best day of my life, so he tried to congratulate me and all. I started explaining about Nancy. We had a few more beers and an afternoon later, I ended up telling him this whole story as well. We talked all of the way through dinner and then decided to hit a karaoke bar; Al thought it would take my mind off my troubles."

"Why would you think that?" asked Zeke.

"You don't karaoke either?" I asked. They shook their heads. "What is it with you guys? I just figured if he was distracted for awhile, it would only be beneficial."

"That's not what you said," piped in Sid. "He was basically calling me out to get me to go, but he was right. It's not like I had anything better to do. So we go, and luckily it wasn't too crowded because, even though I was drunk, I wasn't that drunk. Al then does his professional karaoke song--"

"You have a standard song?" asked Jerry.

"I know, I know. I heard it all yesterday," I said.

"Man, that is so lame," said Jerry.

"He actually did a great job, and it was a decent song," said Sid seemingly out of pity.

"Thank you. I think."

"So, I find a decent song; Al finally convinces me to do it, and I get up on stage."

"In a tuxedo, don't forget," I added.

"I'm a karaoke junkie's wet dream," said Sid.

"Amen to that," I said.

"Oh shit," said Zeke, looking down and shaking his head in disbelief. I think the mental picture was just too tough to take.

"I'm up there, singing the song, and I'm getting into it when the karaoke guy starts grabbing at the microphone stand. What was that all about?" he asked me.

"You were carrying the microphone and the stand; you can't do that. They don't like you messing with their equipment," I said.

"Oh, I guess that makes sense. I had no idea."

"What did you think he wanted?"

"I thought he was going to shut the song down, you know, because of the lyrics."

"What song was it?" asked Jerry.

"XTC, 'Dear God."

"Oh brother," said Zeke.

"Then the guy comes up on stage--"

"This time he was going to shut you down," I said.

"See? I was almost right. So I pushed him off the stage. I wasn't going to get interrupted again. When I saw him signaling security, I knew it was over, and I was just so pissed and angry that I beat the crap out of all of his stuff. Just went to town on it with the microphone stand."

"And then you went to jail?" said Zeke.

"Yeah, then I went to jail."

"And now you owe them five grand?" said Zeke.

"Yep, five grand."

"Well, was that worth it?" said Zeke.

"It was, actually. I can't explain to you how good that felt!" he said with a laugh.

"I don't think this is funny," said Zeke.

"Calm down Zeke, I can handle it," said Sid.

"Oh, I bet. Nancy's not hear to take care of you this time, remember?" said Zeke. "And what were you doing while this was going on?" Zeke asked me.

"I was just watching. I was mesmerized."

"You just let him go?"

"I didn't see any reason to stop him. I was in awe. You have to picture it: he was just nailing this song, you were a little nervous at first, right?"

"Yeah, but--"

"But then he really was getting into it, on stage, lights on him, he's in a tux, he just kills the second stanza! Then the song is all 'I can't believe in, I won't believe in,' and during that pause he knocks the guy off the stage. Then in my head I can hear the rest of the song 'I won't believe in heaven and hell, no saints, no sinners,' but the only sound is in my head because he is just wailing on the equipment on stage. It was surreal. I couldn't move."

"Such a stupid song!" said Zeke. "What a waste of five grand. Oh yeah, five grand you don't even have!"

"Shut the fuck up Zeke! You don't know what you're talking about!"

"We're talking about you throwing five grand out the window, throwing your life out the window."

"Five grand to stand on stage, sing that song and beat that crap to shit, it was priceless."

"It was childish."

"Okay guys, calm down," said Jerry.

"You wanna know what it really was Zeke?" Sid asked.

"Sid--" said Jerry.

"It was five grand so I could get up on stage, and scream to the world 'Fuck God! Fuck Religion!' That was fucking priceless!"

Zeke got up from the table and immediately headed for the exit.

"Zeke, I'm sorry," Sid called after him as he tried to catch up.

I stood up to follow them, but Jerry stopped me. "Let them go," he said. "Let Sid handle it. I've been waiting for this for a long time."

"What?"

Jerry looked around to see if they were on their way back. They were not, so he leaned toward me and began the story.

"You have to understand that my family is pretty religious. We were all brought up with the Church, including mass each and every week, classes after school, the whole nine yards."

"Yeah?" Not that unusual, I thought.

"Zeke is much younger than we are. He's seven years younger than me and eight younger than Sid. At a certain point, Sid and I rebelled against the Church and against our parents. It was teenager stuff, mostly, for me anyway. But Sid...Well, one of Sid's chores was to help Zeke with his homework. One day, when I was around eleven and Sid was twelve, he was reading some bible story to Zeke at the kitchen table, and, suddenly, Sid turns to my Mom and says, 'How can we teach him this crap, Mom? How long can we continue to lie to him?' My Mom was floored. She called my Dad in, and they shuffle me and Zeke out. They have a long talk with Sid. I couldn't really hear what they were saying from the other room, but I know my Mom started crying and would not stop. For a couple of days after that, my house was a mess, but no one really talked about it. After that, my parents sort of let us go. We still had to go to church and whatnot, but there was an understanding even though we never talked about it. They focused that much more on Zeke. They didn't want to lose him too, and he has never wavered. He still goes to church; he still believes."

"Oh."

"And Zeke doesn't know that Sid doesn't believe. Well, he didn't know."

17

Sid came back in a few minutes.

"He wouldn't talk to me," he said.

"What's he doing?" asked Jerry.

"He was just walking, real fast, just trying to get away."

"So, let him go."

"What?"

"I think he finally gets it," said Jerry.

"Oh, ya think?" said Sid sarcastically.

"Hey!" said Jerry.

"Sorry," Sid added quickly.

"Give him a few minutes. He will be back. He's bound to have a lot of questions, and impatience will get the better of him."

"I'm sorry, Jer," he said. "I've been hiding this from him and from myself and from everyone really."

"I figured something else was going on here, you were skimming over the story pretty quickly," said Jerry. "Can I get the adult version please?"

"I'm lost, Jer," said Sid quickly. His eyes began to well up, but he fought back the tears as he looked away. "I realized the other day that I have no idea what I'm doing on the godforsaken planet, and, as everyday passes, I like being here less and less. Fuck!"

"Hey, it's okay," said Jerry.

"After the Padre game, celebrating that night, it just hit me. I have nothing, nothing. I grasp at the air and am shocked to find air. It makes no sense, I know."

"It's okay."

"I shouldn't have said that to Zeke though."

"Zeke's a big boy now, he can handle himself."

"I'm afraid, Jer. I'm afraid all of the time now. I don't know what's going on. I don't have any control over anything."

"Sid," said Jerry as Zeke walked up behind Sid.

"I didn't choose to be this way. I don't understand why I can't just be satisfied with the standard answers like everyone else can. I don't understand why I deluded myself nor why the delusions even bother me. I don't understand why I keep thinking about this great big universe and my itsy teeny tiny place in it. Even though these thoughts scare me, they just eat at me, and I can't make them go away. I can't stand it; I can't live like this. I never asked to be this way. I never wanted to alienate the people close to me. Mom and Dad, Grandma, Nancy. Now Zeke? I never meant to hurt anyone. The last thing I want is for Zeke to go through this too. I don't want him to be like this."

"I'm so sorry, Sid," said Zeke. We were all a little choked up. Sid's anxiety seemed to take up the whole room and overwhelmed me as if it was my own.

"For a moment, I hated you and your disbelief. I even came back here to tell you that," Zeke continued, "but you aren't abandoning me. You aren't abandoning your family. We aren't going anywhere. You aren't going anywhere. We'll get through this." With that, he hugged his brother, and they both started to cry.

18

Because of oodles of ambiguity, religion is one of many issues that Logic and Emotion will never agree upon. Neither side can ever know for sure whether the other is telling the truth since neither side knows the truth in the first place, so it takes a little balance and a lot of trust to reach a resolution. Only by working together can they figure out the common ground, figure out the uncommon ground, and trust each other to bridge the two.

After finally feeling strong enough to return to the subconscious, Emotion and Logic were just in time to witness Sid's breakdown. Impulse was exhausted, his whims satisfied a while ago. Now the fun was over and the responsibility of control weighted on him. Impulse quickly let go of Sid and retreated to the back of the room, however no one immediately stepped up to take control.

For the first time, Logic realized the harm he had caused by avoiding this issue for so long. He realized that Sid was not a body unto himself, and in protecting Sid from this very day, Logic had bulldozed his way through countless other lives with nary a second thought. Sid could see that even Nancy, once Logic's savior, was nothing more than a pawn in the game of control he was playing. With Logic's shortsightedness suddenly cleared, indecision and insecurity now reigned. Logic offered control to Emotion, but Emotion would not accept either!

Emotion had become a whirling vortex of feeling. Fear, anxiety, love, and hatred spun around each other at an increasing rate, leaving Emotion dazed, light headed, and incapable of taking control. Emotion, in fact, was incapable of anything. Emotion was completely unaware of the goings on and just stood there with a blank expression on his face.

Reluctantly, Intuition stepped up to the plate and, after a lifetime of coaching from the sidelines, was forced into the game. Make no mistake, Intuition was not happy about this situation. He grumbled something about 'not his job,' and 'just being here to assist and advise,' and 'not trained for this,' but no one was listening anyway.

19

The four of us sat at the table in silence for a few minutes, reflecting and composing ourselves. I think we all felt a little emotional and didn't know what to say, so no one said anything.

"I'm sorry, Zeke," said Sid finally.

"There's nothing to be sorry about. We're just worried about you."

"I'll be fine."

"Are you sure?"

"I have no idea, but I'm sick of this pity party," said Sid. "We gotta get outta here. Who wants to hit the pool?"

"We didn't bring suits, Sid," said Jerry. "We didn't really pack for a trip."

"Let's go buy some stuff then. They have a ton of shops around here."

"I'm going to run up to the room for a bit," I said.

"You aren't going to ditch us?" asked Sid. "Meet us at the pool?"

"Sure, I'll be down in an hour or so. I have to check my voicemail, email, and make a few phone calls, but I will be down in a bit."

"Cool, see you then."

When I arrived at the pool that afternoon, I could only find Zeke and Jerry sunning themselves in the deck chairs.

"Hey guys! Where's Sid?" I asked.

"He's over there," said Jerry with a point, "floating in the pool. Have a seat."

"He's been out there for awhile, almost the whole time we've been here," said Zeke. "What's he doing out there?"

"He's relaxing. Let him be. Do you want a drink, Al?" asked Jerry.

"Sure, but I can get it."

"I'll get it. Beer? Sid told us to charge it to his room. He doesn't want you paying for anything," said Jerry

"Why not?" I asked.

"Not sure. Guilt maybe," he said as he took off toward the bar to get my drink.

"He doesn't want anyone paying for anything. What's his deal?" asked Zeke. "Where's he getting all of this money?"

"What do you mean?"

"He's in a huge room, right? He keeps adding everything to the bill. How's he going to afford that? He doesn't have the money for that?" said Zeke.

"And the karaoke stuff." I added.

"Exactly."

"I hadn't really thought about it."

"Honestly, it worries me," said Zeke.

"Here you go," said Jerry as he returned with my beer. "Pretty nice day today, pool weather in November, gotta love it."

"How long do we plan on staying, Jerry?" asked Zeke.

"I figure we will stay the night and try to get Sid out of here tomorrow."

"Think he will want to go?" asked Zeke.

"I'm not sure yet, we will see," said Jerry. "When are you going home, Al?"

"Tomorrow as well. I fly out in the morning," I said.

"Where in San Diego do you live?" asked Jerry.

"In Pacific Beach. How about you guys?"

"I live in Cardiff--"

"Where's Sid?" asked Zeke, standing up quickly.

"What?" replied Jerry.

"He's not floating in the pool. Did you see him get out?"

"No, did you?" Jerry asked me.

"No."

"He's probably at the bar or the bathroom," said Jerry. "Relax, Zeke, everything is okay."

"I see him. He's at the bottom of the pool," Zeke said as he jumped in after him. A minute later he and Sid popped up through the water's surface.

"What are you doing?" asked Sid standing four feet deep in water.

"What are you doing?" asked Zeke, trying to drag him out of the pool by the arm.

"Nothing, just sitting on the bottom of the pool."

"I'm not buying that. Come on. Let's get out."

"Lay off."

"Zeke, let him be," said Jerry, still lying in his chair.

"Jerry!" said Zeke.

"Zeke, I'm okay. You don't have to worry about me."

"Sid, please. Will you just get out of the pool? For me?" pleaded Zeke.

"All right, but this is stupid."

Reluctantly, Sid climbed out of the pool and took a seat next to Jerry.

"What were you doing down there?" asked Zeke.

"Just floating!"

"On the bottom? You've been in the pool for like forty minutes."

"That long, really?" asked Sid, looking to Jerry for affirmation.

"At least," confirmed Jerry.

"Wow. But it's not what you think! You're overreacting, okay?"

"Come on Sid, be honest!" pleaded Zeke.

"All right, just listen. I was floating on my back for awhile, just checking things out: there were the kids splashing on the other side of the pool, you guys, the waitresses, and the people at the bar. I was just watching the world and all this commotion going on around the pool, but I'm just floating, and I can't hear anything except the flapping sound of the water because my ears are under water. That and my breathing. It was like I muted the world, and everything was so different that way. After awhile, I felt so relaxed. I can't even explain it; it was like my body almost disappeared. I couldn't feel anything, and my breathing was so loud, pounding around my head. For a bit, everything else left my head except the breathing." Sid had a dreamy, far-away look in his eyes as he told us that last part, but, very quickly, he became self-conscious.

"Then I found myself staring at the sky. No clouds. Just blue, the endless blue. Infinite. I noticed this 30-story monstrosity towering above us. I was like, 'Where did that come from? ,' and it's shooting up towards the sky. So many rooms. So many people, more people than I would ever know in my lifetime. Imagine how many people are in that building. How many people in this city? It's mind boggling.

"And, then, there's me. Just me in the pool. The only sound I hear is my breathing. Then, the sound of my breathing is somehow joined by someone else's breathing, then another, and I started freaking out. Maybe I would never be able to stop hearing it! So, I held my breath and sunk down to the bottom to escape the breathing noise. There was no sound at all, just the watery images floating above me. I closed my eyes, and everything was gone--all sound, all sight--and I was just sitting there, completely weightless and in complete silence. It was glorious. So peaceful. I was about to go up for another breath when Zeke pounced on me!"

"How was I supposed to know? For all I knew you were--" said Zeke before suddenly stopping.

"I was what? Attempting to drown myself in four feet of water?"

"Well, yeah."

"Zeke, I'm not going to kill myself."

"Why not?"

"What?" said Jerry as I choked on my beer.

"Why does everyone keep asking me that?" said Sid with a laugh.

"Zeke! What is wrong with you?" said Jerry.

"Did I tell you that is exactly what Nancy asked me?" Sid asked me. "First my girlfriend and then my brother. What are the odds of that?"

"What did you say to her?" asked Zeke, still very serious.

"I don't remember exactly what I told her, but basically that even though I'm not sure life is worth living, I don't believe any alternatives would be better. I mean, imagine if I came right back and had to do it all over again. From the beginning! No thanks!" said Sid with a laugh. Zeke did not laugh with him.

"What?" asked Sid finally.

"I don't think that's funny. I don't think this is a joking matter," said Zeke.

"Tough shit. You'll get over it," said Sid with a laugh.

Zeke was still not amused.

"Zeke, I'm sorry you don't think it's funny. I'm not trying to insult you or hurt you in any way. I'm just trying to find my own way here, and the best way for me to do that is by laughing."

"I don't see how you can trivialize it or how you can trivialize yourself," said Zeke. "I understand you are going through a dark period right now, but I don't want you to give up, and when you make jokes about it, you seem so resigned, like the inevitable is a foregone conclusion."

"That's just it. By laughing about the inevitable, it inevitably makes the inevitable less inevitable."

"What?" asked Zeke, seeming to speak for all of us.

"I don't even know," said Sid, giggling again. "Everyone dies, right? Laughing about your death takes it from a dark scary place, puts it under the lights, front and center, but in a clown suit. It makes it less daunting and less scary. Does that make sense?"

"I guess so. I just don't understand why you can't believe. I know you hate church and all, and I know you guys think I'm somewhat of a stooge to go to keep going to church, but I always thought, deep down, that you still believed."

"It's not that easy, Zeke."

"I'm sure I've had the some of the same thoughts that you've had, but you're never going to know the answer. So, why ask the question?"

"What if there is a better answer?"

"How will you know?"

"You probably won't."

"See, why then?"

"I don't know why, Zeke. Honestly, I don't. I know what you believe. I know why you believe it, and that's okay, but it doesn't sit well with me, there is this--" Sid paused as he searched for the right words.

"Longing?" I suggested.

"Exactly."

I continued, "The longing inside you is always craving more answers. It's insatiable. This longing doesn't stop with any answer. No answers are good enough. Not one can stop the craving."

"You too?" Jerry asked me.

"A little bit. More so when I was younger," I replied.

"I knew there was a reason we hit it off so well," said Sid excitedly. "What stopped it?"

"Nothing stopped it really. It subsides from time to time then comes back. Sometimes you just get so busy you don't have time to even address it. That's where I've been for awhile."

"But you can't stop it?" asked Sid.

"Not that I know of. No, you can't stop it."

"What?" Zeke asked Sid, picking up on Sid's disappointment.

"You know, I've always thought it was something I could cure and either figure out or get past. I never considered it was here to stay."

"Is that bad?" asked Zeke.

"No, not bad," he said quickly, but he had a suddenly pale look on his face. "It's just different, a different way of looking at it." Sid stood back up. "But I've never known anyone else that thought like I do."

"I'm sure it's more common than you think," I said.

"Is it okay if I go back in the pool for a bit?" he asked Zeke playfully.

"Whatever, asshole," said Zeke.

"I need to float on this one. I will stay at the surface to keep Zeke from going Baywatch on me again."

"Why don't you drown your sorry ass this time?"

"Zeke!" said Jerry. He looked appalled before Sid started laughing.

"That's funny. Now you're getting it," said Sid.

20

The subconscious was rocking with endorphins. Long live endorphins! The body was handing out endless endorphins to everyone, and, like being in a skybox at a ball game with all you can eat and drink, you are obligated to eat and drink as much as you possibly can!

Emotion emerged from his stupor and immediately assumed they were in love! It was the same feeling of course. They are both just chemical reactions caused by endorphins, so Logic and Intuition let Emotion believe whatever he wanted. Emotion pranced around, laughing and dancing with Impulse.

Logic had just finished un-doing his previous patchworks on Sid's psyche, embarking on a new plan to share the psyche. The endorphin attack returned the self-assurance that he had been missing for a day now.

The link between floating and endorphin release had been discovered by some crazy scientists many years ago. Of course, they use an enclosed sensory deprivation chamber for their studies, but I say a Vegas pool on a perfect fall day works a little better, and why quibble? You can't argue with the endorphins! Floating weightlessly eases the workload on one's workaholic brain, causing one's blood pressure, heart rate, and breathing to all slow dramatically. It also allows muscles and body to achieve a complete, deep, pure relaxation. Biochemicals such as adrenaline and other toxins are removed from the bloodstream and replaced by beneficial endorphins. With nobody to look after and free from the majority of its responsibilities, the mind, high on the highest high, wanders waxes, wanes, and wonders, resulting in a heightened sense of learning and creativity.

I liked to believe my love for San Diego was tied to my love for the ocean, or specifically, swimming out past the break and enjoying the up and down floating as the surf goes by harmlessly. Even thinking about it now makes me jones for a quick trip to the beach. Now, I know: it's the endorphins, stupid! It's all endorphins. Endorphins from floating, endorphins from laughing, and endless endorphins from laughing while floating! It makes me sad and it debases my love for the ocean from a romantic notion into mere chemistry, an environment of beakers, rubber gloves and bunson burners! I want to yell "Damn you scientists!" But, of course, I'm a sucker for more information, and in the end, I'm thankful.

21

When Sid went back to floating, Jerry had some questions for me.

"Do you see yourself in Sid? Is that how this played out?"

"Somewhat, maybe."

"You understand what he is going through?"

"Honestly, I don't know. His experience is like a sudden blow to the head. I've always been intrigued by questions like this. Sid seems scared of the questions, and I find them fun."

"Fun?" asked Zeke. "What is fun about this?"

"Just the possibilities. Take what Sid said to me when we first met: there are more stars in the sky than grains of sand on earth. I mean, imagine that!"

"He's asked me that before--"

"He has?" said a surprised Zeke. "He's never asked me anything like that."

"Well, how many times have you gotten really drunk with Sid?"

"Just a couple."

"That's why. I've been drunk with Sid a lot, and every once in awhile something like this will come up. That's why I'm so surprised by his reaction the last couple of days, because these thoughts are not new to him."

"There's a drunk world; there's a sober world, and never the two shall meet!" I said.

"I guess," said Jerry.

"But isn't it a fascinating question!" I said.

"To Sid, it's not," said Jerry.

"That's true. Sid cannot get his hands around the largeness of it all. He can't put it into any perspective. It's just much too large for him. As a result--"

"It scares him," said Jerry.

"Right. Maybe eventually it will affect him like it does me because even though it scares him, he's still fascinated by it. That's why it won't go away."

"At least it's out in the open now," said Jerry.

"When it came up, did you used to avoid the subject or something?" I asked.

"Well, like I said, it only came up when he was really drunk, and the next day he would always seem either ashamed for bringing it up or completely oblivious that it ever happened. So, it's not that we avoided it; it just never went anywhere."

"How does that subject make you feel, Jerry?"

"Infinity doesn't have any effect on me. I'm not the type of person that has these questions about existence. It's unanswerable. That's answer enough for me."

"Let me try this one, do you have a wife and kids?" I asked.

"No, neither."

"Girlfriend?"

"No."

"Okay, let's use your family then. Say Sid, Zeke, and your parents were just killed in a car crash, where do they go?"

"That's terrible!" exclaimed Zeke.

"I know. Sid did that one to me as well. I had to go out and call my wife to make sure she and the kids were okay, but it does cut to the root of the question."

"Wow. He's never gone there with me before," said Jerry, pausing to look out at his brother still floating in the pool. "Honestly, two things pop in my mind. First, my immediate reaction is the hope that they are in a better place, but that is my upbringing rearing its head. Quickly after that, I have the thought that I will see them again someday."

"Like in heaven?" I asked.

"No," he said quickly, and then checked himself after noticing how taken aback Zeke was. "Like Sid, I've rejected most of the beliefs I was brought up with. Does that surprise you Zeke?"

"After everything that has happened today, I sort of expected it, I think. So, you believe in reincarnation then?"

"Yes, it makes more sense to me. Its cyclical nature seems to fit better into the grand scheme of nature."

"So, you still believe in an afterlife," said Zeke.

"Yeah, I guess I do."

"So, that isn't a huge departure," said Zeke.

"True."

"I don't think Sid believes in any of that," said Zeke.

"No, he doesn't," said Jerry.

"A karma system as well?" asked Zeke again.

"Yeah, maybe something like that."

"I know, I know. Nothing specific, nothing organized." said Zeke, greatly over-emphasizing organized.

"Zeke was a Religious Studies major for his first couple of years of college," Jerry said to me.

"Why do you say it like that?" Zeke asked.

"Like what?"

"Like I'm a recovering alcoholic or something?"

"I didn't!"

"You did too!"

"Stop being so defensive," said Jerry condescendingly.

"And you and Sid never had discussions about religion?" I asked in a subtle attempt to change the subject.

"Well, kind of," said Zeke.

"What does that mean?" asked Jerry.

"Well, we always talked about what I was learning. He even read many of my textbooks after I was done with them. Then, we would discuss things, but more like he was a study partner comparing notes. He never asked me any questions like that. He never really even talked about what he believed or what I believe for that matter. We just talked about the ideas."

"I never knew that," said Jerry.

"Not everything revolves around you Jerry," shot back Zeke.

"Whatever, dork!" said Jerry, then they both laughed. "That ties into what you were saying, Al, about it being insatiable."

"Yeah, I know," I said. "It just seems weird to me how he never faced to himself that he didn't believe in any of it."

"You know, now that you said that, most of the time he would just put everything down."

"In front of you?" asked Jerry.

"Well, you know Sid; it was all very subtle."

"That's why I was surprised," said Jerry.

"And about all of the other religions, never one disparaging remark about Christianity. That's why I thought--"

"He was better at hiding some things than others I guess," said Jerry.

"I thought he believed just like I do," said Zeke.

"But why would you think that?" asked Jerry.

"I wanted to believe that. I wanted him to come back. I thought--"

"I know," said Jerry.

After a moment, Zeke turned to me and said, "I thought it would be good for him to have the direction and peace he has so sorely missed."

"What type of things would he say?" asked Jerry.

"Your basic Sid snide remark. Generally some variation of how could anyone believe in that, like everything was so unbelievable."

"Which it can be," I said. "Depending on your perspective."

"I guess, but that gets me back to the point: why bother? You can punch holes into every single philosophical ideal ever invented. Anyone can do it. It's easy because there is no correct answer. That's why it's called The Unanswerable Question. At some point, you are going to have to forget it all and follow your faith."

"Why?" I asked.

"Why what?" Zeke asked back.

"Why do you have to believe in something?" I asked.

"You think that's it?" asked Jerry. "Maybe he's against believing in anything, like believing is the problem."

"Believing isn't the problem," said Sid as he climbed out of the pool. "At least I know that. Part of the reason I was originally so upset was that I had lied to myself. I had allowed myself to believe in something for no other reason than to believe."

"That doesn't make sense to me," said Zeke. "That's what belief is all about."

"Like you said, I spent much of my time disparaging the beliefs of others."

"You heard that?"

"I heard some of it. You drunks are sort of loud," said Sid with a smile. "But it's true, I did do that. I tried not to do it in front of you, but I guess not as much as I thought."

"It's not a big deal, but I still don't--"

"When I first began to question the different kinds of beliefs, I found great satisfaction in the fact that all other beliefs were as tainted as my own. I found it comforting that everyone lied to themselves. Then, I thought I got past it all, believing in things and all; then, I felt. . . not sure what the word is--"

"Superior?" asked Jerry.

"Not really. More like I was an adult on these things and everyone else was a child."

"That's not superior?" asked Jerry.

"I don't think so. A teenager to child relationship is superior. With an adult, you know, it's different."

"You see a bigger picture. You let a child believe in something because it's comforting for them to believe in it at that time, yet you know it's not true," I suggested. "I have kids. I know the feeling well."

"Like that, yes. And then to realize that I too believed in something just for the sake of believing, well, I disgusted myself."

"But you can't get around believing in something," insisted Zeke again.

"But I can," said Sid. "I will."

"Why?"

"Because I'm different."

"Is that what your cork routine has told you?" asked Jerry.

"Don't mock it! I've barely slept for days, and after what, an hour total in the pool or so floating, I've never felt better!"

"Could be the beer kicking in?" mocked Zeke.

"Ha ha, but I didn't even have one smartass."

"Oh, yeah. Champagne then cork boy," countered Jerry.

"How are you different?" I asked.

"I'm not different than everybody else. I'm just different than normal. That's what I meant. Maybe no answer will ever be good enough, just like you said, Al. I thought I was looking for answers. All of these years, all of the books and questions, I thought I was looking for answers, but no matter what answer presented itself or will present itself, I will never believe it."

"And?" Jerry prompted, trying to figure out where he was going with that.

"And nothing. And that's okay. I honestly thought that I needed to believe in something, but I don't."

"So you believe in nothing?" asked Zeke.

"I don't believe. I question. Does questioning everything mean you believe in nothing?"

"Well--"

"Uh--"

"Pretty much, right?" He had us all stumped with that one.

"I'm not so sure, but I really don't know," said Sid. "I know I don't have everything figured out. I know I still have issues to get past, and I feel okay with that."

"That's a lot," said Zeke.

But it could have just been the endorphins.

22

Eventually, we went back up to Sid's room. On the way, he told Jerry and Zeke he was ready to go home, and they decided to leave right away. I tried to say my goodbyes when we got to the elevator, but Sid wanted me to come to his room.

"I'm sure I will see you in San Diego," I said.

"For sure, but I still need one more piece of advice. It'll just take a second."

"Okay."

"There's one thing I haven't told you, I haven't told anyone actually," he continued as we entered his room. This made Zeke very uneasy.

"What now?" he said.

"Nothing bad, I assure you." He went over to the closet and crouched down. "First, let me show you something."

He was fiddling with the safe in the closet for a moment, and then he started throwing wads of cash over his shoulder. Just like in a movie, bound stacks of cash, one after another onto the bed. Zeke was the first to pick one up.

"There are hundreds!"

"I know. Each stack is ten grand."

"Where?" is all that Zeke could get out before he sat down on the bed. "What have you done?"

"How many do you have?" asked an astonished Jerry.

"Last Christmas, I got a bonus from work. I didn't tell anyone about it, I don't even know why, I just cashed it. Then, when I was out here with my buddy for the Super Bowl, I put it all on the Padres."

"To win the West?" asked Jerry.

"No, to win it all."

"You didn't!"

"I did. 120-1 were the odds."

"Oh my God," said Zeke.

"The net of it was $5,238.16"

"There's more than that here though," said Jerry.

"That's how much I bet. That was the net of my bonus."

"How many do you have?" Jerry repeated.

"Forty-five," said Sid.

"$450,000," I said.

"Yes. That's after Uncle Sam takes his cut."

"$400,000!" said Jerry. He too was now sitting. Sid was still emptying the safe.

"$450,348.50. Actually, I spent about a hundred so far, so a little less."

"Holy shit," said Zeke.

"I know," said Sid, finally finished and now standing to look at his handiwork on the bed. "And it's heavy."

"Why cash?" I asked.

"Not sure, but I insisted. It actually worked out well, they said it would take time and put me up in this room."

"Wow."

"But that leads to my question, why I asked Al to join us here in the room. Now what?"

"I know," said Jerry as he jumped up from his chair.

"What?" asked Sid.

Without another word, he ran at the bed and dove on top of four hundred, fifty thousand dollars, rolled over and started to make a snow angel!

"I'm serious."

"How can you be serious right now? There's four hundred thousand dollars on the bed! This is insane!" screamed Jerry.

"You could buy a house," said Zeke.

"That's what I'm looking for," said Sid. "I need direction."

"You could buy a business," I said.

"Fuck that!" screamed Jerry.

"What?" said Zeke.

"Not that they are not perfectly reasonable suggestions, but come on. This isn't something you can decide now. This isn't even something you should consider right now. You need to live just a little first."

"You mean like get a little drunk--" said Sid.

"And get a little crazy," Jerry said.

"And smash up a karaoke machine?" asked Zeke. "Wait, Sid did that last night! Oh yeah, then he went to JAIL, Jerry!"

"I'm serious," said Jerry.

"I am too. I thought we were taking off," asked Zeke.

"No way."

"Why not?" asked Zeke. "Let's just get out of here. Let's just go home."

"Zeke, have you ever done Vegas right?" asked Jerry.

"What does that mean?"

"Every time you have ever been here you have been on a budget," said Jerry. Zeke started to say something, but Jerry kept going. "No, don't start. I'm not picking on you. I'm always on a budget too. Never, not once in our lives, have we had the wherewithal to do whatever we wanted to do here. Vegas is about luxury, and it's about decadence. When we come, we dabble in a little gambling, enjoy the pool and restaurants a little, but, come on, we just scratch the surface. It's like going to church for the fucking wine for crying out loud."

"Jer--" said Sid.

"Oh, he's fine. You know it's true, Zeke. We have never cut lose, abandoned ourselves, and let Vegas rule. I bet you haven't ever lived Vegas either," Jerry said to me.

"He's right. Me too, always on a budget."

"For one night, we can do whatever we want, and we wouldn't even make a noticeable dent in Sid's stash! There's no way we are going home. One night, Zeke. One night is all I ask."

"But its Sid's money," said Zeke.

"Oh. No, Zeke. I'm with Jerry. One night. Anything you want, and it's all on me."

"Al?" Zeke pleaded.

"I'm pretty sure it won't top last night, up until the jail part of course, but I wouldn't mind trying," I said.

"Fine. I'm in, but just one night," said Zeke.

"Just one night. We will leave when we wake tomorrow," agreed Jerry.

"Promise?" asked Zeke.

"Of course," said Jerry.

"Okay, then."

"Now that we have that settled, back to my original question: now what?" said Sid.

"We need suits, and we need a limo," said Jerry quickly.

23

A few hours later, three guys in brand new suits were waiting for me in the hotel lobby.

"Look at those rags. I told you I would buy you a new suit," said Sid.

"What are you talking about? This suit works just fine. It's not even that old."

"I don't know. I'm not sure you can hang with the three of us," said Sid.

"You guys are looking pretty sharp, not tuxedo-wearing, karaoke-singing sharp, but pretty sharp. So, what's the plan?" I asked.

"Jerry has leveraged my newfound status as a big shot gambler, and we have a hotel limo at our disposal for the night, as well as a private room at some swanky new hot spot for dinner."

"Wow!"

"I know. I was pretty impressed too," said Sid.

"It was easy. I told them we would be dropping some big coin at the tables tonight," said Jerry, "and the house always wants their money back."

"What's this place we're going to again?" asked Zeke.

"I don't even remember, but the driver knows where to take us."

"Why do we need a private room?" I asked.

"Why not?" asked Jerry. "It wasn't my idea. I told them we wanted the best. This is what they hooked us up with. Are you guys ready for this?"

"Absolutely," said Sid.

"Seriously, forget about all of the other stuff going on. Forget about the Pads, money, plans, hesitations, and reservations! In one minute, our night starts, and we go as the night takes us!"

"Be real, Jer," said Zeke.

"I am. This is serious! Let it go. Be free."

"I'm ready," said Sid.

"Me too," I said.

"Zeke?" asked Jerry, clearly pushing Zeke's buttons.

"I'm ready," he said.

"Zeke?"

"As the night takes us. . . Count me in."

"Okay, let's go!"

Jerry took us outside and led us to an extremely long, large stretch limo. As Zeke, Sid, and I sat down, we found the champagne had already been opened and poured! This would be a recurring theme on this night.

"I could get used to this!" said Sid.

"Once you have been in enough limos and drank enough champagne, it's just like everything else. You will eventually tire of it," I suggested.

"Really?" asked Zeke.

"I highly doubt it!" I laughed. "That's just what we'll have to tell ourselves tomorrow!"

"If I could always get around like this, I wouldn't hate being in a car," said Sid.

Jerry poked his head in the door.

"Hey, guys. We picked up some extra passengers," he said before disappearing again. Then, one young lady after another started climbing in the limo. These six young ladies were all clearly dressed for a night on the town, and my thoughts began to have a particular Vegas slant, and I was a little nervous. I am, after all, a happily married man. I looked over at Sid, whose face seemed to express the same apprehension. As for Zeke, although I giggle now thinking about it, I cannot put into words the look of horror on his face.

"Guys, I'd like you to meet Linda," said Jerry, motioning to the woman sitting next to him. "She is getting married soon, and this is her bachelorette party. Their limo is a no show, so I've offered to share ours with them. That's my brother Zeke on the left, then Al, and my brother Sid."

"Thanks guys. Welcome to the bachelorette party," said Linda.

"Thanks. Champagne?" I asked. Sid and Zeke were still too stunned to speak.

"Absolutely!" said Linda. "This is Jen, Mandy, my sister Courtney, and that's Maya and Zoey."

I put Sid and Zeke to work passing out glasses of champagne.

"We've been waiting for our limo forever, so I thought this was it," said Linda, "and Jerry, being such a gentlemen, was going to let us have it, but I couldn't do that."

"The driver needs to know where you ladies are going." Jerry asked Linda. As they turned to communicate with the driver, Mandy had a question for Sid.

"What are you guys celebrating?"

"That's a good question," he replied, looking at Zeke and me for help.

"The start of Sid's new singing career," offered Zeke, which made me laugh.

"Really?" asked Maya.

"No, not really," said an annoyed Sid. "We aren't really celebrating anything, just going out for a night on the town."

"So where you guys from?" asked Maya.

"San Diego, how about you?"

"No kidding? Mandy and I live in San Diego," said Maya.

"That's so crazy, because I just met Al yesterday, and of course, he's from San Diego as well," said Sid.

As everyone exchanged which part of San Diego they lived in, I caught Jerry's eye. He gave me a wink and a smile. Now, I didn't really know Jerry at this point, but clearly he was up to something!

We arrived to our destination in what seemed like seconds. One moment we were chatting away and enjoying our champagne, and the next Jerry was yelling, "Everyone out!"

Unbeknown to us, Jerry had also invited the bachelorette party to enjoy the swanky private dinner reservation with us. Zeke was not amused.

"What are you doing?" he asked Jerry.

"Nothing. It's completely innocent."

"I'll bet!"

"She told the driver where they were going; he asked if he should drop us off here first. She was impressed, I told her about the private room and invited them along."

"I know what's going on here."

"What's going on here, Zeke?"

"You know."

"I don't know. I didn't plan any of this. We're going with the flow, as the night takes us Zeke!"

"She's getting married, Jerry," Zeke said.

"I'm aware of that, and I'm not doing anything other than helping make her party something to remember. Is that so bad?"

"This is completely inappropriate!"

"You'd better relax," said Jerry.

"This makes me a little uncomfortable," said Zeke.

"What? Dining with women?" chided Sid.

"Screw you Sid, you know what I mean. And this is the last thing you need."

"Listen. Jerry is right. This is completely innocent. Let's have dinner. We'll get you some more champagne. Let's all relax and go with the flow," said Sid.

"And have fun Zeke. I don't want you ruining Linda's bachelorette party."

"I'm sure you don't."

We were quickly taken to a hidden room that overlooked the rest of the restaurant. It was a big room with a cocktail area as well as a table for dining. The champagne was already iced and poured.

"What a nice room," said Linda. "What are you guys celebrating?"

"Oh, nothing," said Jerry. "Sid had some gambling success, so we are taking advantage of his new connections."

"Excellent. Luck or skill, Sid?" Linda asked.

"What?" he asked.

"Are you a skilled gambler with some system or was it blind luck?"

"Oh, that. No skill whatsoever. Plain dumb luck."

"That counts too," said Mandy.

"What happened to your face?" asked Zoey.

"I thought it was getting better," said Sid. "Does it still look that bad?"

"It looks like you got mugged," said Zoey.

"It's not that bad," said Mandy.

"What happened?" asked Jen.

"Let's just say my mouth was running faster than my feet would normally allow."

"And you got into a fight?" asked Zoey.

"Not really a fight. It was more of a good, old fashioned thrashing!"

"Here in Vegas?" asked Maya.

"No, in Barstow on my way up a couple of days ago."

"Four days, Sid," said Jerry.

"Really? Four days ago?" said an astonished Sid.

"Really," said Jerry. "That was Monday. It's Thursday."

"Wow, time flies when you're having fun. Isn't there anything else we can talk about? When's the wedding?"

With the champagne flowing, it did not take Zeke long to loosen up and enjoy the party that Jerry had created. Soon he and Courtney were locked in conversation at the end of the bar.

"I admit that I like big church weddings," he said.

"Not me. This has been such a hassle, and it's still a month away," said Courtney. "I don't know how much more I can stand. When it's my turn, I'm coming here!"

"You wouldn't," said Zeke. "Your parents would kill you!"

"It's my day. I can do whatever I want," she said.

"Why would you want to do that?"

"It would be so much easier. Besides, I don't think I could stand being the center of attention."

"It's just for a day."

"No, it's not. It lasts for months. From the engagement until the big day, it's always the center of attention. Are your brothers married?"

"No."

"Do you have any sisters?"

"No."

"See? What do you know? Trust me. Elope!"

"I don't know, my mom--"

"She'll get over it. Please pass the champagne."

"Are you even old enough to be drinking?" he asked as he grabbed it for her.

"I'm definitely older than you are. Maybe I should be the one asking that question," she said.

Dinner was a blur of food, endless bottles of champagne, and lots of laughter.

"What should we do now?" asked Linda.

"What did you guys have planned?" asked Jerry.

"We just planned on going club hopping, but this has been a lot more fun."

"I know what we should do," said Sid.

"Let me guess, karaoke?" said Maya.

"What?!" said Sid.

"That's a great idea!" I said to the horror of Sid, Zeke, and Jerry.

"I wasn't sure it was you until we got in here and saw your face," said Maya. "We saw you singing at the bar last night."

"It's you, right?" asked Zoey.

"Well, yeah, but--"

"You owe me a buck," said Mandy to Zoey.

"This is too funny," said Jerry. "Zeke and I missed yesterday's big show."

"Unfortunately," said Zeke.

"No kidding. So, tell us from your perspective what happened. The story Al tells is a little over the top," said Jerry.

"I don't think you can go over the top on this one," said Jen.

"We're basically just getting started for the night, a little happy hour before dinner, right," said Maya. "Then Zoey points out this guy in a tuxedo standing on the stage and blinking into the lights. The first thing you notice is the tux."

"We thought you were some wannabe lounge singer in that tux," said Zoey with a giggle.

"Oh, yeah. We were so ready to heckle the crap out of you," continued Maya, "but the second thing you notice is that you don't have a clue what's going on."

"My first time," offered Sid.

"Clearly!" said Maya. "So, we backed off a bit, and when you started, it was pretty bad at first."

"I bet Mandy a buck you wouldn't even finish," said Zoey. "It was bad."

"This is much more like what I pictured it to be," said Jerry.

"But then he started getting into it," said Maya. "He's actually singing, feeling more comfortable on the stage, and the tux actually started to work in his favor."

"See? I told you so," I said.

"Then, he just lost it!" said Zoey, and started dancing around the room swinging an imaginary bat. "Beat the entire stage to crap!"

"Oh my, I turned to take a sip of my drink, and when I turn back, the karaoke guy is on the ground, security is rushing the stage, and you were just going to town on the speakers and equipment!" said Maya. "They drag him down, cuff him, and march him out of there."

"I, for one, was glad karaoke was done for the night," laughed Linda.

"You had the funniest look on your face when they were marching you out of there," said Mandy. "You would think that there would be some remorse, some oh-my-god-what-have-I-done look on your face, but it looked like you were amused by the whole thing."

"You can't even imagine how good that felt!" said Sid.

"Why in the world would you do that though?" asked Zoey.

"It was the end of a few long days," he started. "I don't really know, I wasn't really thinking I guess."

"Where did they take you?"

"The drunk tank," said Sid. "Yes, I spent last night in jail."

"Oh my God," said Zoey with a laugh.

"I know. Needless to say, karaoke is not in the cards for tonight. In fact, I'm not allowed to sing karaoke within the city limits for two more years."

"Shut up," said Maya.

"Okay, so that may be more of a personal limit I've placed on myself," confessed Sid.

"With good reason," said Zoey.

"Who won the bet then?" asked Jerry.

"That's right," exclaimed Mandy. "You owe me a buck, he finished the song."

"He didn't! They dragged him to the ground before the song was over."

"The singing part was over," said Mandy.

"I agree," I said.

"Are you sure?" said Zoey.

"I can still see it now; I'm pretty sure. Once the lyrics ended, he dropped the microphone stand and then they tackled him," said Mandy. "Were you bowing at the end?"

"Maybe, I don't know."

"I can't decide if I wish I would have seen it or I'm glad I wasn't there," said Zeke.

"I wish I could have seen it," said Jerry.

"You totally would rather have seen it; it was epic!" said Courtney.

"I tried to get the surveillance video from the hotel," said Jerry.

"You did not," said Sid.

"I did," said Jerry. "They were kissing my ass so badly as I set this dinner up, I thought it wouldn't hurt to ask."

"What did they say?" I asked.

"Something standard line about never releasing any footage to anyone in order to respect the privacy of their guests."

"You should've offered them money," I said.

"I did that too," laughed Jerry.

"Thank goodness you didn't get it. Let's just let it die here," said Sid.

"I doubt that will ever happen," said Maya.

"You can rest assured of that," said Jerry.

"Enough about me, I would like to make a toast to the man that made this all possible," said Sid as he raised his glass. "To Jerry!"

"To Jerry!" said the group.

"So backing up a bit, what did you want to do next?" Jerry said to Sid.

"Oh yeah," said Sid. With that, he stood up and called Jerry over to the corner of the room.

"What is it?" asked Maya.

"After that little episode, I don't think I want to tell you," he said. "You will have to wait and see."

Jerry was on his phone the entire limo trip back to the Luxor. Once we arrived, Jerry and Sid led the group to the casino floor and a private roulette table. There were bottles of champagne in stands situated around the table and chips laid out at each station.

"Roulette?" said Linda.

"Roulette!" said Sid.

"And champagne?" I offered.

"Come on, it will be fun. How often can you play on the casino floor, completely uninhibited, with no fear of losing your shirt."

"Maybe I want to lose my shirt," said Jen.

"Whoa now!" said Jerry.

"I've staked everyone to begin with," Sid continued. "So you don't have to worry about the money, we are already playing with the house's money."

"I'm game," said Mandy.

"Me too," said Courtney. She dragged Zeke to the table to sit down, and everyone found a spot around the table.

"Some people will tell you the key to roulette is to play the odds. The thirds, black or red, blah blah blah. But the key to roulette is in the numbers! You have to know the magic number. A single number pays what?" Sid asked the dealer.

"36-1," said the dealer.

"36-1!" said Sid.

"Thanks, Sid. I think most of us have played roulette before," said Jerry.

"Just trying to be helpful."

"It remains to be seen whether that is helpful."

"Ah yes, doubting Jerry," said Sid. "We'll just see then."

Sid moved a stack of chips to the red 19 circle and said "Yes, let's play."

"19? That's your big strategy?" said Jerry.

"What's 19?" asked Courtney.

"T Gwynn," said Zeke.

"Anthony Keith Gwynn!" said Sid.

"Who?" said Courtney.

"Tony Gwynn?" Zeke repeated. "You don't know who Tony Gwynn is?"

"No," she said.

"He's just the greatest Padre ever!" said Sid.

"Padres, that's baseball right?" said Courtney.

"That's baseball!" said Sid, still excited about his strategy. "Who just won the World Series?"

"I'm going to guess the Padres," said Courtney.

"Right you are!" said Sid. "And do you know how many times the Padres have won the World Series?"

"Do I have to guess?" said Courtney.

"Just one," said Mandy.

"That's right! Just one time. In the 40 year history of Padre baseball, one time. The stars aligned, the fates intervened, and destiny's darling, those San Diego Padres, win it all. So you know what that means?"

"No."

"Just tag along for the ride. Follow the magic. Let's play Padres!"

"You seriously don't know who Tony Gwynn is?" an astounded Zeke asked Courtney.

"Oh get over it already!"

19 did not win the first spin, nor any of the next four, but Sid did not waver and kept to his strategy.

"10," said the dealer.

"Damn! Gary Sheffield! That would have been a good one," said Sid.

"Bip Roberts," said Jerry.

"Oh, even better!" said Sid.

"What number was he?" asked Courtney.

"They're both number 10," said Zeke.

"Thinking about branching out?" I asked.

"Thinking about it," he said.

"Destiny's a little slow on the draw," said Mandy.

"Destiny, and her sister Fate, usually aren't very kind."

"What does that mean?" said Mandy.

"I don't know, isn't that from a movie?" he asked.

"I don't think so," she said.

"Maybe some book I read. Destiny is the stuff of movies and stories; it isn't real."

"You don't think?"

"You do?"

"Sure, it's a romantic notion, but I like to think there's something to it."

"Same with him," he said pointing to me. "Do you want to know the only reason I did karaoke last night? It's his fault!"

"I take full responsibility," I said, "but, in my defense, you were in a casino bar drinking in a tuxedo well before karaoke came up. Some things just happen."

"Destiny?" he countered.

"Look at how many things had to happen for you to be at that place, at that time," I said. "Coincidence? I think not!"

"What kind of things?" asked Mandy.

"Oh, we don't want to get into all of that," he said.

"What were you doing in a tuxedo?" she asked.

"Ugh," he sighed.

"You don't have to tell us if it makes you uncomfortable," she said.

"I spontaneously proposed to my girlfriend that morning. It was totally in the heat of the moment. Put the tux on and surprised her, and she said no."

"Wow."

"She had just come in because of the fight and this," he said pointing to his face. "I had pretty much ruined things already, and it isn't right for either of us."

"How could she say no?" asked Courtney.

"Pretty easily," said Sid.

"That sounds romantic as hell. On those grounds alone, she should have said yes," said Courtney.

"It's a lot more complicated than that," he said, "and she's not the spur-of-the-moment type, so that part actually didn't work in my favor. . . at all."

For a moment, the group was stunned silent. The roulette wheel continued clicketing while the casino noise filled the silence, but it felt like you could have heard a pin drop.

"So, the moral is that sometimes you see destiny, but that's just the spin your mind is giving you. Whether it be for romantic or poignant reasons, you see destiny, but it just isn't there."

"19 is the winner," said the dealer.

"Yes!! T Gwynn baby!" erupted Sid as he jumped out of his chair and ran around the table high-fiving everyone.

"Oh my God, how much did he win?" said Zeke.

"Over $700," said Jerry.

"See?!" said Sid pointing at Jerry.

"Destiny's darling," said Mandy.

"Padres! Padres! Padres!" Sid started to chant. Soon the rest of the table was chanting as well.

"Maybe you just haven't seen far enough down the destiny line!" I said.

"Maybe you're right!"

Much later, our group was down to five. Linda and Jerry were in the bar; they'd had enough gambling. Maya, Zoey and Jen went to the club to finally go dancing. Zeke, Courtney, Sid, Mandy, and I were still playing. Sid was up thousands of dollars. He'd hit with 19 half a dozen times at least before he started branching out and won with Dave Winfield (31), Adrian Gonzalez (23), and even Sixto Lexcano (14).

"Zeke, are you in or out?" asked Sid.

"What?" said Zeke, turning his attention away from Courtney.

"Are you playing?"

"Oh, that."

"It seems Zeke is on his last legs," chided Sid.

"You're one to talk."

"Now that I'm moving back to San Diego, we're going to have to go out drinking more often. Your tolerance is embarrassing."

"Screw you, Sid."

"When are you moving back to San Diego?" asked Mandy.

"Probably tomorrow unless I keep winning; then I may never leave! Anyone else playing 19 this time?"

"I'm playing Archangelo Cianfrocco," said Zeke.

"Who?" said a number of us.

"Archi Cianfrocco," repeated Zeke.

"What the hell number was he?" asked Sid.

"You don't know?" asked Zeke.

"No, do you?"

"Nope," he laughed. "Guess I'll play 19 with ya!"

"No more bets," waived an infinitely patient dealer.

"That's going to bug me," said Sid. "What number was he?"

"29," said the dealer.

"Shit, I think that was his number!"

"See? fate." said Mandy.

"Oh, enough out of you."

"I'm playing 2," said Zeke. "Did you get that one?"

"Alan Wiggins," said Sid.

"Yes! Alan Wiggins," said Zeke.

"Okay, I will ask again. Who is Alan Wiggins?" said Courtney.

"A poor, lost soul who used to play second base for the Padres in the eighties. Here's to Alan Wiggins!" said Sid.

A toast to Alan Wiggins. We had toasted nearly every player that had ever played for the Padres at this point!

"Want to know what I don't understand?" said Mandy.

"Sure," said Sid.

"I don't see why you don't just run with it. The Padres won it all; you won big; 19 is kicking some serious ass. Destiny is on a roll."

"Destiny again."

"Yes again."

"Okay. Still, that's just what you want to see."

"I don't want to see it. It's more than that, can't you just feel it?"

"I don't. What's the difference between destiny and luck?"

"I don't know. What?"

"Luck also has a bad side, a down side that equalizes the good side. With destiny, it's only about happily-ever-afters."

"Yeah, so?"

"So, most of the time, there aren't happily-ever-afters. Destiny is a fairy tale. Life is no fairy tale. Life is a bitch."

"It depends on how you look at it I guess," she said. "Perception. Who's to say?"

"Perception, exactly. Who's ever to say?"

"Exactly," she said. She seemed pleased with herself while Sid seemed utterly confused.

"Everyone's playing 19 this time," said Sid.

"Okay," said Zeke, and everyone put the necessary chips on the red 19 circle.

"I'll show you," whispered Sid to Mandy as he placed a stack of chips on the red 19 circle.

"Oh yeah?" she responded, as she did the same. "I can handle it. Can you?"

Destiny's darling did it again. As the big winner was announced, the table jumped up, and suddenly a crowd was around us also cheering. I started up the Padre chant again and began to high five the roped off crowd circling the table. I circled the table to Zeke and Sid's side, but I was left hanging. Mandy was kissing Sid, and Courtney was kissing Zeke.

"See? Destiny." Mandy said, her arms around his neck.

"Oh my!" he said. He took both her hands in his and looked deeply into her eyes. "I have to go to the bathroom," he said quickly and walked away.

"What happened?" Jerry asked as he suddenly appeared by my side.

"He did it again, but this time we were all playing," I said.

"19? Again?" asked Jerry.

"Again," I said.

"Unbelievable."

"I've never seen anything like this," said the dealer. "Do you think you guys are still playing?"

"I think we better wrap this up now," said Jerry. "Where's he going?"

"Bathroom," said Mandy.

"You okay?" I asked Mandy.

"Sure, I have to go to the bathroom too," she said.

"I will go with you," said Courtney, giving Zeke another kiss before following Mandy.

"What is going on around here?" asked Jerry.

"Just going with the flow, Jer," said Zeke, unable to contain the huge grin on his face.

Zeke and I joined Jerry and Linda at the bar, our mountain of loot in tow.

"What do we do with this?" asked Zeke.

"That's up to Sid I guess," said Jerry.

"No no. I'm gambling mine, can I just take my rack to another table?" he asked.

"Oh. No, take it over there to the cashier. They will give you cash for it, and you can go to another table or whatever."

Mandy and Courtney walked up.

"The old folks are slowing down," Zeke said to Courtney. "Are you done?"

"Definitely not!" she said. With that, they took their racks and walked arm in arm towards the cashier. Mandy sat down with us.

"You kissed him?" Linda immediately asked.

"Not now," she said.

"What were you thinking?"

"What's his story?" she asked Jerry, ignoring Linda's question. "Did he really just break up with his girlfriend?"

"Yes, he did yesterday after almost three years. And because it's obvious something is going on with you two, I am going to tell you this: Sid is having a personal crisis at the moment."

"I gathered that," she said.

"He just decided to move back to San Diego. He just quit his job. He just broke up with his girlfriend. He's not in a good place right now."

"I know, I know," she said.

As she took this in, he continued. "I like you. I really do, but don't go too far too fast. He's not ready for anything right now."

I nodded in agreement with Jerry.

"I know it looks bad. I just broke up with my boyfriend. I'm in no shape to be pursuing this either, but…"

"I know he's a lot of fun, and he's really putting on a show tonight," started Jerry.

"But it's not about tonight," she said.

"It's not?" said Jerry.

"No. It's about last night," she said.

"Last night?" Jerry repeated.

"At karaoke?" Linda offered.

"Yes," said Mandy.

Since that didn't seem to make sense, the table was quiet.

"He's up there on stage, all beat up, in that tux, with this angst etched into his face and pouring into his voice as he belts out that song. And of all songs, that song, I can't believe in you. It was the most beautiful thing I've ever seen."

Everyone was still quiet, so after a minute she continued.

"You have to understand that I have been thinking about this guy in a tux singing that song all last night and all day today, replaying it in my head over and over. And today I'm in a limo with him, then I'm talking to him, arguing with him."

"Kissing him," added Linda with a smile.

"Yeah," she said, clearly embarrassed. "It's just so overwhelming."

"And all of the talk about destiny," I said.

"Hell ya!"

"I wish there was something I could say," said Jerry.

"I know," she said. "It's stupid."

"And we've been drunk for days," added Linda.

"Yeah," said Mandy, still visibly conflicted.

"There you are," I said to Sid as he approached us.

"Hey guys," he said, with a quick smile at Mandy. "Where're Zeke and Courtney off to?"

"They aren't done gambling yet," said Jerry.

"So where are they going?"

"What do you mean?" said Linda.

"I mean, I just saw them get into a cab," said Sid.

"What?" said Jerry.

"I was outside, just to get some damn fresh air, and as I was coming back in they were getting into a cab."

"That's weird. They didn't say anything to us," said Jerry.

"Who cares?" said Linda. "Let's go dancing."

After sitting, eating, gambling and drinking champagne for hours, dancing felt glorious. We were inundated with stimuli: the music blaring; the lights glaring and the crowd swaying. The mind was overpowered, we couldn't think and we couldn't talk. Quickly the mind shuts down and the music takes control. After a short time floating with the crowd, I felt completely refreshed. Most likely, it was an endorphin induced euphoria.

Sid and Mandy danced, but stuck in the middle of the dance floor with the rest of us, they could not talk about the kiss or anything else. The longer we danced, the more self-conscious each seemed to become. No longer drunk enough just to react, each was clearly more reserved towards the other, and each was probably confused for different reasons. Mandy was overwhelmed by the sequence of events that led to her meeting Sid, and Sid by literally everything that had happened during the last five days.

After we'd had enough dancing, we returned to the bar that had become the hub of our stay at the Luxor. Jerry, Sid, and I sat resting in a table at the bar. The ladies would venture out and stop by from time to time.

"I'm beginning to worry about Zeke." said Sid.

"They have been gone for quite a long time," said Linda.

"I wonder where they are at,"

"Didn't they just walk by?" said Jen.

"No. Why?"

"I was over at the slots, and they walked by, heading this way."

"We didn't see them. How long ago was that?"

"Like 15 minutes."

"They must have gone upstairs."

"Food sounds like a good idea," said Jerry.

"You guys want to go get something to eat?" Sid asked. "I'm buying!"

We went upstairs to find Zeke and Courtney and to get some food. We looked everywhere, but they were nowhere to be found.

"Maybe they went into one of these shows," suggested Maya.

"I just don't see a young couple having a blast gambling," said Jerry

"Among other things," added Mandy.

"Yeah, I just don't see them sitting down for a show," said Jerry.

"Me either," said Linda. "Court wouldn't be into that."

"Maybe they went upstairs," said Zoey.

"No," said Sid quickly.

"How can you be sure?" Linda seemed suddenly concerned.

"That's not Zeke's style," said Sid.

"They definitely didn't go upstairs," said Jerry.

"They could have gone back down without us seeing them," I suggested.

"Unless," said Sid.

"You thinking what I'm thinking?" said Jerry.

"That they're in that chapel," said Sid.

"That's what I'm thinking," said Jerry.

"They wouldn't," said Maya.

"Court would," said Linda.

"I'll be right back," said Jerry, and he was back way too quickly.

"They won't tell me if anyone is in the chapel."

"Did you tell them we are looking for someone?"

"Yeah,"

"We can't just barge in there," I said.

"Why not?" said Linda.

"What if it isn't them?" I said. "That would be kind of awful."

"We could, no one in there would be able to stop us, but should we? I see what you are saying."

"Yeah," I said.

"Do we have any other choice?" asked Sid.

"They must have gone back downstairs," said Mandy.

"You guys are overreacting," said Zoey.

"No," said Sid. "They're in there."

"How can you be so sure?" Linda said.

"Because that is something I would do," said Sid.

"I object!" said Jerry as we burst into the chapel. It was them, and based on the way everyone was standing around, either the ceremony was already done or we were early.

"This isn't a courtroom; you can't object," said the pastor. "You are not even supposed to be in here!"

"What are you doing here?" said Zeke.

"What are you doing here?" countered Jerry.

"I'm afraid you are going to have to leave," said the pastor.

"He's our brother," said Jerry.

"And my sister," added Linda.

"We're all going," said Jerry.

"No we're not," said Zeke.

"What do you think you are doing?" said Jerry.

"Just going with the flow, Jerry, as the night takes us like you said. Well, this has been the greatest night of my life, and I ended up here."

"Court, I need to talk to you," said Linda.

"No, I know what I'm doing," said Courtney.

"You don't have any idea what you are doing," said Linda. "You don't even know Zeke."

"I've spent the last eight hours with Zeke. I think I know enough. He's the most romantic person I've ever met!"

"Don't be stupid."

"Hey!" said both Courtney and Zeke.

"She's right," said Jerry. "This is idiotic!"

"Screw you, Jerry. We know what we're doing."

Things were quickly spiraling out of control until Sid stepped into the middle of it all.

"Can I just say something?" said Sid, stepping between everyone with is arms raised, like something from a hostage crisis movie. After a few nods and stopping Zeke from interrupting with a point of his finger before he could say anything, he continued. "I'm not saying don't do it; just don't do it blindly. This has been a great night. Many things have happened, most of which none of us ever expected, and that surprise, that happy surprise, can sometimes seem like something else. Two nights ago, I had a night like this with my girlfriend of three years, and I ended up in the same place you did Zeke. I wanted that feeling to last forever so I know exactly what you're feeling."

"The next night he was in jail. Think about that, Courtney," said Linda.

"Whoa, brutal," said Sid. "Can I finish?"

"Sorry Sid," said Linda.

"Sometimes we get so caught up in the wonder of life, the real details get lost. We get so caught up in the feelings that we do what seems necessary to sustain those feelings without ever figuring out the true cause of those feelings. We attempt to latch on to the hope because it's been so long since we felt hope. We had a great night, and, not to be cruel, but it's not because of Courtney alone, Zeke, or

Zeke for you Courtney. Or me or Jerry or any of us. It's because of all of us, and because of the circumstances. It was a great night, fun, wild, random, exciting, but, really, nothing more than that. Nothing magical, and the feelings that are driving your decisions right now maybe gone just as quickly as they came."

Sid seemed to be speaking as much to himself as to Mandy or anyone else in the room.

"I mean, how is the rest of your relationship supposed to live up to tonight?"

"Since I know you won't sleep on it, how about you at least eat on it?" said Jerry. "Let's go grab some food. If you still want to get married, we will all come back, and you will have our full support."

"What?" said Linda.

Jerry looked at her with a cock of his head.

"Linda?" said Courtney. "Would you give us your support?"

Reluctantly Linda agreed. "Sure. If you still want to go through with it, I will support you."

Halfway though a very early breakfast, Zeke and Courtney together decided it was too soon. The emotional roller coaster had taken its toll on everyone, and, after breakfast the groups said their goodbyes. Zeke and Courtney exchanged information, promising to talk later that same day. Mandy also gave Sid her number and email address and asked him to give her a call once he got settled. After a round of hugs, the night was over.

I went to the airport an hour later in the same limo we used all night. Everyone else went to bed. Zeke did not wake up until six that next evening, and when he did, Sid and Jerry were ready to go. This time, it was Jerry convincing Zeke that it was time to go. They stayed the night in Barstow before making it back to San Diego the next day.

San Diego

24

When Sid returned to San Diego with his brothers, he was determined to rebuild his life and find his purpose. Zeke took him in at his apartment while he sorted everything out. Through the rest of November, he continued to struggle. Everyone had heard about his fortune, so in any situation with family or friends he had to answer the what-are-you-going-to-do question over and over. Not just with the money, but with his new life back in San Diego. Everyone had advice; everyone had an investment opportunity; and everyone also had a daughter, sister, friend or niece that would be perfect for him.

By December, he had retreated further from everyone. He stayed in Zeke's apartment the majority of the time, occasionally going out with Zeke, Jerry, or myself to a bar for a drink, but always just one of us at a time. I tried to invite him over to my house for dinner a couple of times, and Zeke tried to get him to attend a couple of church functions, but he did not want to be out in social situations.

It was early January before Sid had finally answered his real 'what now?' question. At Zeke's urging, he bought a loft in downtown San Diego, which he now shares with Zeke. I put him in touch with a business broker, and, almost immediately, he bought himself a bar. It was also downtown, but off the beaten path, among retail shops. It was just a little dive that you would hardly notice if you were walking by. When he finally got the keys in early March, he asked Zeke, Jerry, and I to come see it.

"Keep your eyes closed?" He said to Jerry and Zeke as he fussed with the lock on the door.

"Sid, I'm looking right at it, I still have no idea what's inside," said Jerry.

"Jerry! Come on," pleaded Sid.

"All right, fine," said Jerry reluctantly.

Sid shuffled them inside, we all stood in the dark for a minute until Sid found the lights.

"Ta-da!" he said as he flipped on the lights.

"Geez, it's tiny," said Jerry.

"A bar?" asked Zeke. It was a valid question. Between the dim lighting and the lack of any decorations on the wall, the only defining feature in the place was a bar that ran along the back wall.

"How much did you pay for this?" asked Zeke.

"Three hundred thousand. Since I paid cash, I got it at a discount."

"Do you have any money left?" exclaimed Zeke.

"That's a discount?" exclaimed Jerry.

"Yeah, we have a full liquor license, that's cheap. And no, I'm pretty much tapped out."

"You spent it all on this?" said Zeke.

"Come on, this place is great. The ballpark is only five blocks away. It's just the right size, this is exactly what I was looking for. I can't believe I found it so fast."

"That was pretty amazing," I said.

"You knew?" Jerry asked me.

"He set me up with the broker so I told him when I bought it. I had to tell someone, and I wanted to surprise you guys."

"But why a bar?" asked Zeke.

"I have to do something, right? I just can't lie around forever. You were telling me to invest the money. I invested in this."

"I was thinking mutual funds or bonds or something. Not this," said Zeke.

"You don't like it?" said Sid.

"But there will be no foot traffic going past this place at night," Jerry said, echoing my sentiments from a month ago. "How will you get people in?"

"The place is tiny. How many people do I need to pull in?"

"You will need a lot of people to stay in business," said Jerry, and again, this was my thought exactly.

"You worry too much; it'll be great."

"You're running a business now, Sid," said Jerry. "You should worry. These are the things you should be thinking about. You've got rent; you will have employees; you have alcohol costs and insurance. All of these things need to be covered by your customers."

"I know that, Jer. Relax. People are going to love this place."

"How are they going to love it unless they come in? I don't mean to be a jerk on your big day or anything, but I don't see how you are going to attract business."

"This is not just a business."

"What are you talking about?" asked Jerry.

"I'm not looking to make a ton of money here. I don't even want a ton of people coming in here. We will have an awesome jukebox, and it will be a lot of fun, but I want this place to be very distinct. I want to cater to a small, loyal clientele."

"Like who?"

"Well, baseball fans for one. That's why I wanted to be close to the ballpark."

"But everyone goes to Gaslamp after the games. That's over there, Sid," said Jerry with an emphatic point.

"Let's hear him out. Who else?" asked Zeke.

"I don't know yet. Just people like me, people who are looking for a place to fit in, people who have gotten lost in this crazy world."

"Who's that, Sid?" asked Jerry. "How will they find out about this place?"

"I don't know," answered Sid honestly and not one bit affected by the questions.

"What are they going to do here? What will make this place any different from any other bar?"

"I have no idea. I have no idea how it will work, but I know it will work."

"Sid," said Jerry.

"Look, I appreciate your input. Al said these same things to me a month ago, and I still don't have them worked out, but that is why I brought you all out here. I need help. I'm counting on your help. So let's figure out the answers to all these questions you have. I want to open as soon as possible to be ready for opening day."

"When is that?" asked Zeke.

"April seventh."

"That's three weeks away," said Jerry. "Okay, first things first, what are you going to call it?"

"I don't know."

"Geez, Sid. We need something to work with here."

"At some point it will name itself. Let's just call it 'The Bar' for now."

"The Bar? A big sign that says 'The Bar'?"

"No sign. I don't want to waste any money on a sign right now. I barely have enough for a juke box."

"You don't have any cushion?" asked Jerry.

"Oh, yeah. I have what Al told me to put away for operations, but I can't touch that."

"Oh, good," Jerry sighed.

"See, it's not as bad as you think," said Sid. "Cheer up."

"I can't believe you aren't nervous at all," said Jerry. "You just dropped a ton of money for this place. You have no plan whatsoever. You don't even have a name. Why are you so sure this will work?"

"Because I'm going to make it work."

25

Even though the four voiced subconscious of Sid was completed months ago, all was not smoothing sailing on the SS Sid. Logic's grand gesture kept the peace for a couple days, but after that the battle over the direction returned. Distrust and doubt do not disappear overnight. They are not washed clean away like magic, endorphins or not.

Emotion and Intuition did not feel ready to commit to anything and were unwilling to go along with the rush demanded by Logic and Impulse. Emotion was recovering from the love that was lost, and while he could understand that it was for the best, the heartbreak made him gun-shy to begin anything of substance. The mere suggestion of a new love interest brought on a crying fit and a violent shift in the opposite direction. Intuition deemed patience to be the best answer. Patience and time would point in the right direction, but of course, that is what Intuition always said. Inaction is the same as indecision, and old habits die hard.

Both of them were driving Logic crazy. Logic and Impulse liked every idea presented to Sid during his first months back in San Diego equally and would have liked to pursue each and every one although for completely different reasons. Logic demanded that the money be put to good use and right away before it got wasted so they could get life back on track. 'Forget about the past,' Logic demanded; 'now is the time for action.' Impulse agreed on action. That last night in Vegas showed Impulse a whole new world. Impulse was fascinated by the myriad of possibilities. So endless, so free they could be, all they had to do was act. Action. Action. Action.

With no clear course, Sid stalled. Maybe this, stalled as they were, caused a floating sensation and another attack of endorphins. Maybe a month of indecision had all four desperate for an answer. Who knows? But when the idea for the bar first popped up, each was on board. Logic thought it was a sound investment, a wise use of the money in a business that will never go out of style. Impulse hoped that every night would be untamed Vegas all over again. Emotion was ready to mingle amongst the world again to renew his search for meaning and love everlasting. And Intuition, well Intuition just thought it was time for action.

26

When the bar opened two weeks later, the only thing that had changed was a jukebox in one corner and a TV mounted up in the other corner. Sid opened the place himself everyday, and, with the help Jerry and I offered on the busy nights, Sid didn't even have to hire anyone since it was so small. Actually, with the six people, counting me, that even showed up on a regular basis, there wasn't that much work to do.

"Man, I thought for sure more people would stop by before the games," I said to Sid.

"Hey, we got two," said Sid. "Guys, this is my friend, Al. Al, this is Mike and Scott."

"Are you guys going to the game?" I asked.

"Yeah. Usually we just tailgate, but it was a last minute thing," said Scott.

"I never knew this place was here," said Mike.

"Yeah, it's only been open a couple weeks now," I said.

"At least you've got the game on. It's hard to find a place where you can just sidle up to a bar and watch the ballgame. This is nice."

Since these were exactly the kind of people Sid was hoping to frequent his bar, he fed them some free beer and they hung out a lot longer than they expected.

"Are you guys ever going to the game? What inning is it?"

"It's top of six already," said Scott.

"This wouldn't be the first time we had tickets to a game, were at the game, and did not make it in," laughed Mike.

"And the tickets were free anyway," said Scott.

"Middle of the sixth. We need some points!" said Mike.

"Rally shot?" asked Scott.

"You know it," said Mike.

"What's a rally shot?" asked Sid.

"We need two shots of tequila, what kind of tequila do you have?" asked Scott.

"What kind do you want?"

"Patrón, Cabo Wabo, Don Julio," said Scott

"Cazadores, Tradićional, heck, Hornitos if you've got it," said Mike.

"Patrón?" asked Sid.

"Good, two, and quick, we have to do it before the end of the commercials," said Scott.

"Let's make it three, Al looks like he needs a shot," said Mike. He must have seen me salivating. "Three always works best."

Mike was fishing is his pocket for something and pulled out a small sandwich bag.

"What is that?"

"Pepperoncini. I never leave home without them," said Mike as he handed one each to Scott and me.

"Ready," said Scott.

"Ready," said Mike.

"Go Padres," they said in unison and downed the shots. I followed suit, but stopped when they popped the pepperoncinis in their mouths.

"Pepperoncini chaser?" I asked. "Why?"

"You want the Pads to score, right?" said Scott. I nodded yes. "Then do it."

"All right! Now sit back and watch the magic work," said Mike.

Sid was curious. "Why the pepperoncini?"

"The official Padre rally shot is tequila chased with a pepperoncini," said Scott.

"How did that get started?"

"The rally shot started in '98. I don't remember how the pepperoncini got started, but I know you started that part. You and your pepperoncini," said Scott, pointing to Mike.

"I don't quite remember either. I think we did normal tequila shots for a rally one time, but it didn't work so we tried a different chaser, something like that. Or maybe we ran out of limes," said Mike, barely taking his eyes off of the TV, where the leadoff runner was already on second. "It works a heck of a lot better than a lime. Didn't it just go real smooth with the shot?"

"It did actually," I said.

"Really?" said Sid.

"You should try it?" I said.

"Not yet, wait until next inning. You can't do one in the middle of the inning," said Mike. "Anyway, it worked. We kept doing it; it kept working, and the Pads made the World Series."

"Do you always carry some with you?"

"Sometimes. I just happened to save these from lunch after Scott invited me. You just never know when you need them. Yes!" Runners were now on first and third in the ballgame. "We went to a sports bar for that first game of the World Series that year, and they didn't have any so we used jalapeños, and that turned out badly. So, if it's a big game, yes, I always bring my own."

"Bingo! See? It's like magic!" said Scott after a sac fly drove the run home.

"Awesome," said Sid. "I will try that tomorrow."

"Tomorrow? Are you kidding me? We are doing another one next inning!" said Scott. "But put that bottle on ice or in the freezer. Colder is always better."

"Another one?"

"Sure. You want to win, right?" said Scott.

"It's only June," I said.

"We know that. It's early, but you can't think about tomorrow in the middle of the game today. You have to be 100% focused on the game right now," said Scott.

"Shoot. There's always tomorrow," I said.

"There is no tomorrow. There is only today," said Sid, as he put the tequila on ice.

Sid got hooked onto the rally shot. He started buying huge jars of pepperoncini at the warehouse store and did rally shots in every close Padre game.

"Middle of the sixth. Let's go, boys," said Sid. He lined up shot glasses for the group of us: Me, Sid, Zeke, and Mike and Scott, our two regulars. As he filled each with tequila, I grabbed the jar of pepperoncinis. To my surprise, it only had a couple left.

"Sid, do you have another jar. This one is about empty."

"How can that be? They come like a thousand to a jar or something."

"We sort of do a lot of rally shots, Sid."

"Hurry up," shouted Mike.

"What are we going to do?" Sid asked.

"I don't know," I said in a panic.

"I got it, pass out some of those saltines," said Zeke.

"Why?"

"We don't have time for that, the inning is about to start. Pass them out and follow my lead," said Zeke. The saltines were passed out quickly and everyone did their shot before the commercial ended then turned to look at Zeke. He took his saltine, broke it in half, held it up in the air, and said "Body and blood of Christ. Amen." Everyone followed suit. It took three batters for the Padres to score and take the lead.

"That's screwed up," said Scott.

"That was a bit messed up," said Zeke.

"They scored didn't they?" said Mike.

"I thought it was sheer genius. We are going to have to work that into the rotation," said Sid.

When Jerry showed up a few hours later, it was just Sid, Zeke, and I getting ready to shut down.

"How'd it go tonight?"

"5-3, Padres," said Sid.

"You know that's not what I meant."

"I know. It was slow. Just Scott, Mike, and a few stragglers, but we have an awesome new rally shot."

"Really? What now?" Jerry was a skeptic when it came to the power of the rally shot. I was a devout believer.

"Tell him, Zeke."

"No, you tell him, Sid."

"We ran out of pepperoncini, so the kid here grabs a saltine and does communion after the shot."

"No way."

"Pads promptly score 2. Ballgame's over."

"Wow."

"I know. I'm thinking we should have a regular sixth inning rally shot, and do that routine each time."

"Sid, I've been thinking about it, and I don't think we should do it anymore," said Zeke.

"Why not?"

"Because it's wrong. I don't know what I was thinking."

"Nonsense. That was beautiful."

"I'm serious."

"You were caught up in the moment, in the game. You didn't mean any harm by it. It doesn't change your beliefs at all."

"I shouldn't mock my religion, Sid."

"You were praying, weren't you? Praying for a run, praying to the big Padre in the sky. That's all."

"I'm not going to rationalize my way out of it, Sid."

"Then you go on wallowing in your guilt. That was the first time I had communion and actually got something out of it."

"Take it easy, Sid," said Jerry.

"No. Don't get me wrong. I respect his beliefs. I don't want to upset him, but that was awesome. We're doing it again."

"How can you do that?" asked Zeke.

"I don't believe, Zeke. That's not news anymore. What's more, mocking beliefs makes me laugh. I think it's hilarious, and don't you dare go all Christian on me, Zeke. It was fun. It had no meaning. Let it go."

"You can't go around offending people's beliefs."

"Why not? Do Christians worry about their beliefs offending anyone? Do they care one iota about anyone else's beliefs? Of course not, they think it's their duty to shove that crap down our throats. Do unto others, Zeke? I say turnabout is fair play."

"Is that how it's, Sid?" asked Zeke, standing up suddenly and making his way to leave. He made it all of the way to the door before Sid relented.

"Don't go."

"I can't stay. I can't believe I started this."

"I'm sorry, don't go. Maybe I'm going too far. Trying to force my beliefs on other people is just as wrong."

"Then you won't do it anymore?"

Sid was silent for a second.

"All right, listen. I won't do it when you're around, okay?"

"And that's supposed to make it okay?'

"It's more meeting halfway. What do you think?"

"I think that's crap."

"Come on, please. Zeke, that was so awesome, I want to do it again."

"Sid--"

"Come on. It's for the Padres. Can we do it for the Padres?"

"When you put it like that, fine. Do it for the Padres," said Zeke reluctantly. What self respecting Padre fan could have resisted?

27

Zeke and Sid were getting along all right as roommates, but Zeke stayed away from the bar for a while. He spent more and more time at his parents' and at church. Sid called it his penance for what he had done and held no ill will towards Zeke, but I think, secretly, Sid was happy about it because every game, home or away, TV or radio, he did the special sixth inning rally shot.

Rally shots were done all night during the Padre games and occasionally during other games as people tried to adopt the tradition for their teams. Mike and Scott still stuck to their original pepperoncini routine. For them, switching after so many years would have been sacrilegious, but almost everyone else went the saltine route, and almost everyone in the bar participated in the sixth inning rally shot.

We had a number of people who tried to stop in just for the shot, but since it's hard to tell exactly when the sixth comes around, they always ended up staying. One guy, following an east coast day game via the internet from his office, stopped by in his suit and tie on his lunch break for a shot.

That's not the only change that was taking place inside the bar. Over the next few weeks, Sid added quite a few new decorations to the bar. The first one was a prayer station complete with the pad for kneeling, about two dozen candleholders, and a slotted box for donations that he found at an antique store. He set it up along the wall next to the jukebox, and every night there were a few more candles lit.

Next, he found pictures of Jesus, Buddha, Confucius, Moses, Mohammed, Jackie Robinson, Elvis, and the Padres Swinging Friar, and put them all in one big frame together in a collage and mounted it above the prayer station. The bar was taking on an identity of its own. It had just took a little time as Sid predicted, and slowly people started noticing, and more people started coming. The next time Jerry brought Zeke came in, he was astounded by how busy the bar was, and, considering it was a Wednesday night, so was I.

The Pads were at home against the Giants, one of their most hated division rivals, so the crowd was pretty fired up. By the top of the sixth, people were placing orders for their rally shots.

"I'm gong to need three today, Sid," said John, pointing to his friends.

"All righty. No saltines today, just pepperoncini," said Sid.

"Oh, come on," said John. "It's their first time. They have to have the saltines."

"Sorry, all out."

Quickly the word spread through the bar, you would have thought the bar ran out of alcohol! The outrage was loud and pure. Then Scott, our original regular, sitting at the end of the bar with Zeke and Jerry, almost started a riot.

"What are you talking about, Sid. I see the saltines right there."

After the loud cheer subsided, Sid stuck to his guns. "Sorry, folks. No saltines today."

A saltines chant started for a moment, but that was interrupted by rage when the game went to commercial. It was the middle of the sixth with less than two minutes to go. When a shot glass missed Sid's head by inches and slammed into the wall behind the bar, Jerry ran around the bar, dug out the saltines, and tossed them at the crowd like he was feeding ravenous dogs ready to eat his brother, which they may have. It was completely quiet immediately, followed by a unified, almost reverent "body and blood of Christ. Amen" and a loud cheer as the game came back from commercial.

Sid gave Zeke a sheepish shoulder shrug as if to say sorry, but he couldn't hide his smile. He couldn't help himself; he just loved it.

"Zeke, I'm sorry about the rally shot tonight," said Sid later. "I really tried to skip tonight, but--"

"There was nothing you could do about tonight, but don't you think this is a little out of control?"

"I think he's right, Sid. I thought they were going to mess you up," said Jerry.

"And look at all of this stuff, Sid. What are you trying to do here?"

"I know you think a lot of this stuff is sacrilegious, Zeke, and I can't really argue that it's not, but it's drawing people together here. It's creating something larger than ourselves and connecting to it. I'm not trying to debase your religion or any religion. I'm just trying to create a community where I fit in, and where other people like me can fit in and feel there is some goodness in this godforsaken world. Doesn't that seem like a good thing?"

"Sounds like you want to start your own church," said Zeke.

"That's pretty much exactly what I want to do," he said.

"But--"

"Now listen. I know it sounds weird, but I don't think I'm alone out there. All through the holidays I kept thinking about how tough this time of year is, how the suicide rate rises. You know, all of that stuff you hear. And you know what? That's me. If I didn't have you guys, that's me. If not dead, then out on the street, drunk and alone."

"Sid," said Zeke.

"Don't kid yourself. You were expecting me to do it in Vegas. You know it's true. We have a world dividing itself into ever smaller factions. It's a world where not only do you not know your neighbor, but you don't even want to know your neighbor. If you don't have your family or friends close by, you can easily get lost. On top of that, if you don't have religion to turn to, it's a quick snowball's ride to hell.

"And it's more than that. You don't only lose those connections you lose the belief that there's good in the world. It's gone, sitting next to hope on that snowball. You can't imagine how tough it is for me to admit there are some positive things about religion. It's like admitting the Yankees had a good team in '98. It just burns so bad inside to even think it, but each week at church you see a bunch of people like you, people who still believe in goodness. When you let go of church, you don't see goodness in people on a regular basis, you just see the crap of everyday existence because not too far underneath the surface people are mean and selfish."

"I know. I know. That's why you should go to church!" said Zeke.

"But don't you get it? I can't pick and chose the pieces I want to believe in, and I can't possibly overlook the hypocrisy that fills me with hate when I think about it. The door of religion is closed for me. Can you understand that?"

"No. You are so close here. You recognize the goodness that extends to all people, and you are trying to recreate the exact same thing! How can it fill you with hate? How can you hate that?"

"It's not the same."

"How is it different?"

"There is no God for one," he said quickly and paused as if waiting for a reaction. I understood that Sid had always been afraid of influencing Zeke. It seemed like he liked that Zeke still believed, like he was jealous of the peace and stability it lent to his life, but, maybe for the first time, he realized it was Zeke trying to influence him, trying to bring him back to their church. Zeke had, in fact, ever since he was a little kid, always been trying to bring Sid back to their church.

"We aren't worshiping any deity. We will not meet out of obligation. We will not be forced to believe in one truth. We will not believe in truth. We will not hold our beliefs above the beliefs of anyone else, nor force these beliefs onto anyone else. We will be open, instead of closed, to new ideas. We will embrace differences instead of fear them. We will not be coerced or degraded with guilt. And we will not try to convert anyone."

With that last one he paused again. Zeke wouldn't even look at him.

"Zeke, I know you want me to come back. All of the books you leave laying around the apartment, the church calendar on the fridge for crying out loud, but you have to accept it's not going to happen, and that's no big deal."

"I'm just worried about you."

"And you have every right to be. You are my brother and nothing will ever change that, but I can't be who you want me to be. I know you expect more from me, but I can only be who I am. I'm just trying to be who I am."

"And this is who you want to be?"

"This is who I am. This is who I've always been, and it's probably why I boarded it all up on the inside. The person I am is offensive to the ones I love, but I can't hide it anymore."

"I understand."

"Are you sure?"

"Yeah, sure."

"We okay then?"

"Yeah, sure."

"Good."

But even I could tell that Zeke was not okay.

28

A week later, I received a surprising phone call from Zeke asking if he could talk to me. I stopped by the apartment the next day on my way to 'work' at the bar.

"Thanks for coming, Al."

"Sure thing. How's it going?" I asked.

"Going all right I guess."

"How is Courtney doing?"

"She's doing great. I'm going to see her in a couple of weeks, and she will be coming out in a month or so."

"That's great."

"Yeah. Long distance is tough, but what are you gonna do?" he said with a smile.

"Yeah. So what's this all about? I was surprised you called."

"I know and sorry about being so cryptic, but I need to talk to someone, and most of the people I normally talk to wouldn't get it."

"How so?"

"That's probably not the best way to put it; it's more that I don't want to talk to them about this. I don't want anyone to know."

"Okay."

"Not Sid either. I thought about talking to Jerry, but he would just tell Sid. You won't tell Sid, will you?"

"Not if you don't want me to."

"Good."

"What is it?"

"I don't know how to deal with Sid."

"What do you mean, 'deal with Sid?'"

"I feel very uncomfortable in the bar. I'm very uncomfortable about the bar in general. I feel like a hypocrite every time I step in there, and I hate that feeling, and everyday he asks me if I'm stopping by. What can I say?"

"Man."

"I mean, it's only four blocks away that it really cuts down on my excuses. I used church for a while, but now he pulls up and prints the calendar off of the internet to post it on the fridge for me so he knows what's going on and when. He's trying to be supportive of me, or something, in the hope that I will be supportive of him."

"Probably."

"I use work, he says, 'just for a bit.' I use not wanting to drink, he says 'don't have a drink.' He has a comeback for everything."

"Why do you think he wants you there so bad?"

"He's afraid of pushing me away."

"Is he?"

"Pushing me away? No."

"Are you sure?"

"Well, maybe a little. I can't avoid him. We live together. I see him everyday. His anti-church thing bugs me so much I can't even explain it."

"You have to tell him," I said matter-of-factly.

"No way!"

"What do you want from me here, Zeke?"

"Do you think this is just a phase?"

"No, I don't."

"What do you think is going on with him?"

"You are asking the wrong person."

"Tell me, please."

"I think he has stumbled upon what will be the greatest church of the 21st century."

"Come on, seriously."

"I'm completely serious. You have to see it from our side, Zeke. You feel good when you leave the bar and not just because of the buzz. Spiritually, you feel better. You feel happy. You almost feel hopeful. It's pretty powerful for people like us who don't have that normally. I stop by almost everyday, and it seems there are a lot of people like Sid and me out there and more everyday."

"It's just a bar."

"No! It's so much more than that. You have to open your eyes to it though."

"That's crazy."

"Check this out. I was talking to this guy yesterday. We were chitchatting during the game then he goes over to the candelabrum and kneels down, and he's there for quite some time. Finally, he comes back and sits back down, then says to me, 'I haven't done that for a long time.' I asked what, and he says, 'Prayed. Not for the game or anything, but for my grandmother who is sick.' I must have looked at him funny or something, because then he says, 'but I prayed to the Friar.' He felt better about himself after saying a prayer for his grandmother to the Padres' Swinging Friar. Can you believe that?"

"That's stupid."

"It's not. It's cathartic. Sid has created something that is giving people peace. It's the most beautiful thing in the world, and it's not just one guy. Every night all of those candles are lit. It's like thirty bucks a night that thing rakes in, and Sid saves it all in what he calls the Poor Shooter's fund. He only takes money out if he gives out a rally shot that someone can't pay for. It's just crazy. Every night people say thank you to Sid like he just saved their lives! And the alcohol only has a little bit to do with that."

"But--"

"Listen, I can't tell you anything. If you don't want to see it, you don't want to see it. You should just tell him you don't want to go to the bar anymore. He will understand. I know this is hard on you, and you are feeling something akin to what he was feeling on the other side of the fence, but the feeling is the same. You can tell him. He will understand. It won't be a big deal."

"What am I supposed to tell him?"

"Tell him the truth. Tell him that the bar disrupts your peace. It's causing you grief, guilt, whatever."

"Are you sure?"

"Positive."

"It won't upset him?"

"Not in the least."

"Maybe I will then. I would have to tell him eventually anyway."

"Right. You know what though?"

"What?"

"What you should really try to do is go back just one more time and watch the people. Some people are just at a bar having fun; that's true, but some people are getting a lot more out of it. You can spot them if you try. You don't even have to talk to them. You can see it in their faces. It's as if a great weight is being lifted from their shoulders, and it's just beautiful."

29

A week or so later Zeke did come back to the bar, and, boy, did he ever pick the right day to come. It was Memorial Day so Jerry and he were off work and joined Sid and I at the bar in the late afternoon. The bar was quiet, just us four and Scott and Mike.

The Cardinals were in town so, unfortunately, downtown was awash in a sea of red. It wasn't long before a couple of fans wandered into our haven.

"Afternoon, gentlemen. Can I get you a drink?" said Sid to the two men that had paused in the doorway.

"Is this a bar?"

"Yes, it is. Have a seat. I'm Sid. What can I get ya?"

"Thank heaven. A couple of Buds would be great."

Sid retrieved two bottles of Budweiser, and the two men took a seat in the middle of the bar. "Here you go."

"Thank you. I'm Billy; this is Joe."

"Nice to meet you. I take it you're going to the game tonight."

"Yep. We just got in yesterday for a vacation with the families," said Joe. "Bill and I snuck out to catch a game and check out your ballpark. Has it always been downtown?"

"No. It used to be in Mission Valley, more inland. They've just been downtown since 2004."

"Wow, pretty new then. It looks pretty nice from the outside. We had a good look at it when we flew into town," said Billy.

"I told you, we went to the other one last time we were here," said Joe.

"I didn't doubt you. I was just asking," said Billy.

"Where are you guys from?"

"St. Louis. Can't you tell," snickered Joe.

"You never know. Doesn't most of the Midwest consider the Cards their team?"

"Yeah, that's true. They come from all over, but we're two genuine articles, born and raised in St. Louis," said Billy.

"It makes it tough to get a ticket sometimes. I was surprised we were able to get tickets to the game today. You guys don't sell out games?" said Joe.

"We will towards the end of the season if they stay in the hunt. Where you sitting?"

"Toyota Terrace, Section 212," said Billy.

"That's a club level. Those are usually the last seats to go. They're a little pricey," said Sid. "There will probably be high-30s at the game today."

"How many does it hold?" asked Joe.

"42, I think, depending on the Park at the Park."

"42? And you can't sell out on a holiday weekend?" said Joe.

"Most people are at the beach this weekend. It's basically the first week of summer."

"What's this about a park?" asked Billy.

"There's a park just outside center field. You can get a general admission ticket and hang out there or at other standing room only places throughout the ballpark. It's pretty popular. People will sit on the hill, picnic really, and watch the game or watch the big screen back there. Lots of kids running around."

"That's sort of neat," said Billy.

A man came up to the bar on the other side of Joe. "Sid, I'm going to the game tonight, can I do a rally shot before the game?"

"You most certainly may, Wade."

He turned to his female companion and asked "Do you want one?" She held her hand up and said a quick, almost startled "No."

"Just one," he then said to Sid. Sid poured the shot, put a saltine on top like a cover and handed it to Wade. Wade did his shot, raised the saltine up in the air, broke it and said "body and blood of Christ. Amen!" before eating his saltine. He then threw a ten spot down on the bar and made his way to leave.

"Thanks, Sid. You're a life saver."

"You're welcome. Go Padres!"

"Go Padres!"

"What was that all about?" asked Joe.

"That's a rally shot."

"A what?" asked Joe.

"A rally shot. You do a shot before the Padres come up to bat, usually in the later innings, to help the Padres score some runs."

"Does it work?" asked Billy.

"Sure, most of the time. Actually, Scott and Mike over here invented it, and we adopted it at the bar. Now we do a regular shot in the middle of the sixth."

"What about the cracker thing?" asked Joe.

"Oh that. We practice religious tolerance at my bar."

"Did you hear what he said?" Joe asked Billy.

"No, I didn't," said Billy.

"He said 'body and blood of Christ. Amen'," said Joe. "He acted like he was going to communion or something."

"That ain't right!" said Billy.

"I know! What kind of place are you running here?"

"To quote my mother, 'to each his own.'"

"And what's that?" asked an increasing belligerent Joe.

"That's a prayer station."

"That's what I thought. What's it doing in a bar?"

"I like to think of my bar as sort of a 'church for wayward souls.'"

"And that? Is that what I think it is?"

"That's new actually, do you like it?"

"What?" asked Billy.

"Those tablets," said Joe, pointing to Al's new decoration on the wall. "They supposed to be the Ten Commandments?"

"Something like that, but not commandments. We don't really believe in commandments. Maybe the Ten Suggestions, or the Ten Guidelines. One our regulars made those. It's actually a write board. So, we can put whatever on it and change it as we see fit. I just think that's so clever." As Sid was talking, Joe had gone over to see what was written on the tablets.

"Shit," said Joe. "Listen to this crap, Bill: I believe in today; I believe in using the father's name in vain; I believe there is no after life so leave it all on the table today; I believe in doing the right thing because it's the right thing to do and not for fear of eternal retribution; I believe baseball is the greatest game of all time. Finally, one I can understand. These yours?" he asked Sid.

"No. It was a collective effort. When Hank brought it in on Friday I think. The bar sort of had fun with it."

"And there's twelve."

"So far. It's a work in progress, really. There were 20 at one point. It's not set in stone or anything."

"Not funny."

"What else does it say?" asked Billy.

"Crap. I believe in the soothing power of alcohol; I believe you have to lead by example; I believe in tolerance; I don't believe life is worth living, but I don't believe in any alternatives either--"

"That one was mine," said Sid.

"I believe life is suffering so ease suffering anyway possible; accept your irrelevance; accept others even if they can't accept their irrelevance. Do you think all of this is funny?"

"I thing a few of them are very funny."

"No, I mean all of this. Is this some joke?" said Joe.

"Not at all. It's completely serious."

"Why are you doing this? Why do you have all of this stuff?"

"It just happened. I put in a couple things. People keep bringing in more things. I didn't set out to create this place the way it is. It just happened."

"Now I see why no one's here," said Joe. "Good people aren't going to put up with this shit. I swear, kids these days. Let's go, Bill. You should get all of this crap outta here. Maybe you would have a decent bar."

"Have a great game," said Sid.

"Come back in the sixth, pin head," I said. I don't know how Sid kept his calm; I was pissed off.

"What?" said Joe.

"Many people enjoy this shit just the way it is. Come back in the sixth, you'll see."

"Al," said Sid, giving me the calm down arm wave.

"Fuck you, asshole!" screamed Billy.

"Bunch of stupid shit heads," mumbled Joe as they walked out.

"Can you believe those guys?" I said.

"Al, no need to get them all riled up."

"Sorry, Sid. I'm just so pissed."

"How did you stay so calm?" asked Jerry.

"I get people like that in here all the time during the days. You guys aren't here then. I'm used to it."

"How can you take that crap?" I asked.

"I'm no more right than they are. Everyone has their beliefs. Everyone is entitled to their beliefs. They weren't doing any harm."

"Do you think they'll come back?" asked Zeke.

"No," I said.

"I doubt it. They'll go to the game, and then go back to their families. You really need to calm down, Al," said Sid.

"Man, I'm so fired up right now. Give me a rally shot," I said.

30

Part of the reason behind Sid's calm exterior was the ball of confusion frolicking in his interior. As he stayed calm, Logic and Emotion both stewed over each Cardinal insult, the pot getting increasingly hotter, both ready to brawl. While no one can spout righteous indignation like Emotion, Logic was certainly no slouch!

Logic was preparing a treatise on the idiocy and infancy of their beliefs, leading with "I used to believe in the Tooth Fairy and Santa Claus as well, but I was six and then I grew up!" Intuition was trying to stay in control and trying to keep Logic even-keeled, and, incredibly, looked to Emotion for assistance. As if. Emotion liked Logic's start, but quickly tired of the rhetoric and did not feel it had enough wallop to it anyway. Emotion had one response in mind, and it led with a left jab. Action, they demanded, now is the time for action!

"You thought those Cardinals were bad. Of all the short sighted, egotistical voices I have heard in my time, you three are the worst!" said a new voice. "Arguing up here like the fate of the entire world rests on your response. Emotion, predictably, getting worked up and flying off the handle at a few insults, desperate to fight and kick some serious good old boy ass! Why? All to protect your over inflated sense of self worth?"

Logic had to laugh.

"What are you laughing at? Just look at you, Logic," the new voice continued. "All ready to prove how smart you are and how stupid and childish they are for their belief. You just can't wait to wallow in your intellectual superiority. Just who do you think you are?"

"And poor Intuition is stuck in the middle, struggling as usual," the voice said with mock pity. "Not sure if words or action are demanded by the situation, your genetic course work unfortunately ended with 'Response to Physical Harm 101' so you never made it to attacks of the personal and rhetorical realm. Apparently a graduate level course, eh?"

"You all realize you are nothing but biochemical phenomena, right? You are chain reactions and a conditioned response to stimuli. You don't really exist in the spiritual sense of the word, not at all. Why have you not learned this yet? Your very existence is the stuff of lab rats and syringes. It's inconsequential and futile."

Intuition, Logic and Emotion stopped, startled by the new voice. They were startled by the affront of the words, startled by the sting of the insight, but mostly startled by a new voice joining their exclusive group. They looked at Impulse, who gave a sheepish look and shrug of his shoulders to say "not me."

"Where is that voice coming from?" they all wondered, because as quickly as it came, it disappeared.

31

They did come back in the sixth inning just like I asked them to. The bar was packed and Zeke, Jerry, and I were swamped with rally shot orders. I didn't notice them come in, and by the time Zeke pointed them out to me, Sid was already talking to them by the door. I left Jerry and Zeke behind the bar to see what was going on.

"Right is right. This is wrong," said Billy. They had obviously found some place else to drink, and liquid courage seemed to have brought them back.

"Says who? Says you? Says the Church?" said Sid.

"Damn right says the Church! Read the Bible--"

"I don't believe in the Bible, I don't believe in your church, get it? This is still America, isn't it?"

"Free speech does not mean you can desecrate the church. You can't do this stuff," said Joe, waiving at the prayer station and tablets.

"I think that's exactly what it means. Relax, will ya? We aren't hurting anyone. We aren't campaigning in the streets or knocking on doors. It's completely harmless."

"It's wrong, just like Bill here said. You kids think you can just do and say whatever you want. You have no respect. Sure, it's still America, but America is about respect, and that starts with God. Many generations worked hard to create this great country. You can't just spit on that with your disbelief."

"It's disrespect, he's right," piped Billy.

"Its religion, disrespect comes with the territory."

"I can't believe you can stand here so cavalierly about this," said a frustrated Billy. "You are insulting my church with this crap. Do you understand that?"

"I understand and I apologize. It's all very new and probably overzealous, but not meant as an insult. It's not about you or your religion."

"The hell it isn't. You damn well mean to insult someone with this 'body and blood' crap. You are insulting the Lord every time you do it," said Joe.

"It's harmless. We're just a community of like-minded people. We have Christians, Muslims, Jews, Buddhists, and even Hindis that come here. Jim's a Yankee fan for crying out loud. Everyone is welcome, and look how much fun everyone is having! Look at all of these people. No one else seems to mind."

"Just a bunch of dumb kids who don't know any better. You slackers just goof off and expect the world to change for you. Well, I have news for you: things are fine the way they are. You guys are the problem. Not us. We aren't changing."

"I wouldn't expect you to change. It's not about you. Why do you expect us to change?" said Sid, still as calm as twelve inch surf at two minute intervals.

"I expect you to get in line," said Joe.

"Again, who's line? We can argue all day, but, at the end of the day, none of us matter. None of this matters."

"Bullshit!" said Joe, his frustration growing exponentially at Sid's complete calm.

"Like I said before, believe what you want to believe. Just give us our space to find our way. I'm not alone. This is the future here. This is the next generation. This is for them, not you."

"You have got to put a stop to this," Billy piped in. "I'm serious. You stop them or we will."

"What does that mean?"

"You know what that means."

"No, I don't really. Are you going to take everyone's shot away? Their crackers? Kick everyone out of the bar?"

"No."

"Are you going to have my liquor license revoked?"

"We could. We have powerful friends."

"Right, I bet you do."

"We're not kidding around here, Sid," said Joe with a point to Sid's chest.

"Whatever. If you guys can't peacefully coexist with the rest of us then maybe you should just leave."

"Hear me real good, Sid. You know what you are doing is wrong. I see that. You'd better get your shit together and fix this," said Joe, with another point to Sid's chest.

"All right, out you go," said Sid.

Zeke came up behind me and asked, "What's going on?"

"The Cardinals were just leaving," I said, trying to sound as tough as possible.

"We're going, but I'm taking this," said Joe as he grabbed the tablet white board off of the wall.

"The fuck you are!" I yelled, but Sid held me back as they scampered out of the bar.

"Let them go, Al," said Sid.

"What was that all about?" asked Zeke.

"They were a little bent about the rally shots and the decorations," said Sid.

"He threatened you, Sid," I exclaimed. "He was poking you too!"

"What?" said Zeke.

"They're harmless. What are they going to do?" Sid said, shrugging it off. "A couple of guys on vacation with their families got a little drunk. It's totally harmless."

"They stole your Ten Commandments," said Zeke.

"Guidelines, remember? We don't believe in commandments here. We don't judge; we tolerate all, even those that disagree with us."

Even after we closed the bar down, emotions were still running high.

"What are you going to do?" asked Zeke.

"What do you mean?"

"Can't you see this is only going to get worse!"

"What do you expect me to do? Hire a bouncer or something?"

"These are very core, fundamental beliefs you are mocking. People will get upset."

"Angry is more like it," added Jerry.

"You can't push people's buttons and expect no reaction. You are messing with big things, Sid," said Zeke.

"You don't think I understand that, Zeke. You don't think I know exactly how deep these feelings run and how fragile you can be if they are disrupted in anyway? I understand that. Believe me, I understand that better than anyone."

"Why then? What are you trying to do here? Change the world?"

"I'm not trying to change the world, Zeke. I'm just trying to survive it."

"So, why are you pushing your luck?"

"We're just a little place. I don't have a sign. I don't advertise. Don't you think you are blowing this out of proportion?" pleaded Sid, looking at Jerry and I for support.

"I'm with Zeke on this one Sid," said Jerry. "This time it was a couple of tourists. You don't know who it could be next time. I know you're having fun and all, but it's just a bar, it's not worth your life."

"Geez, I can't believe this. Just a bar, that's right. It's just a bar!"

"Sid, be reasonable," said Zeke.

"You've got to tone it down," said Jerry. "Just tone it down a bit. Why does it have to be so--?"

"Offensive?" said Zeke.

"This is not about you Zeke," said Sid. "It may be offensive to you, but not to everyone."

"It's pushing it," said Jerry.

"Oh geez. Let it go. It's late. I'm going home, can you guys lock up?"

"I can," I said.

"Let me go with you," said Zeke.

"No," said Sid. "I'm just going to walk for a bit."

"Sid?"

"I'll be fine."

32

Logic, Emotion, Intuition and Impulse were astounded by what had happened. When the Cardinals reappeared, Logic was ready for action. His soliloquy included the link between religion and community as a way to tie everyone to a common history, ideology, peaceful coexistence.

Emotion, concluding that no fighting was going to take place, still wanted some insults thrown around: "Let's let the Lord handle it," and "At some point down the road, your generation will die off, my generation will age and mellow, and new generations will be born. No one ever changes their beliefs. Beliefs die as era's die. Paradigm shifts just take time, so sit back and relax."

But that voice came back. And not only that, it completely dominated the situation. Again! Logic and Emotion were forcibly shoved aside, and this new voice maneuvered through the entire scene.

"You don't get it?" the voice mocked. "Still think every situation demands a response by the self? If the self does not exist, what's the point of its perception of events? What's the point of its response? There's no point insulting these people. There's no point trying to educate these people. It will not change anything. They do not matter and never have. You do not matter and never have. The only thing changing around here is your awareness of not mattering!"

"But Emotion is right about one thing: ideas die with eras as generations pass. Only you don't seem to understand that this era of yours will also die," the voice continued. "Let's evolve here, people! Intuition clearly will be the first one to go. You have an entire history of conditioned responses at your disposal, but in a world changing so rapidly, you are now eight steps behind the pace and only falling farther behind. He waits pathetically with flight and fight responses of a long gone era, but he's just a bystander doing nothing in the here and now."

"Maybe you still have a place in this world, Emotion, but too bad you are so easily duped into superstitious fantasies playing on vanity and so ready to believe in you own self-importance. You're so eager to defend your preferred position at the center of everything. Emotion is lucky. Even an irrelevant world consists entirely of interpersonal relationships otherwise there would be no purpose for him either."

"And Logic, aren't you the conceited one considering your youth and relatively recent arrival on the scene? So intelligent is Logic, just ask him. He loves playing with his rhetorical toys and creating steadfast rules, always condemning superstition as fallacy and attempting to advance his own ideas. Isn't it clever how he uses the superstitions of others when it suits him and to prove his own importance? Logic, instead of pursing evermore rules, instead of wasting time trying to get around the steadfastness of these rules when they no longer suit you, why not just seek to understand and accept the variety of life? Alas, stupid question. Logic is anti-variety. Logic believes in one right answer, one way, one truth, one self. One is the closest number to zero. Pontificate on that for awhile, oh-self-indulgent one!"

But when Jerry and Zeke started in, Logic and Emotion started up again. Irrelevant or not, surely a response in this situation was appropriate? This wasn't an impersonal interaction with strangers. Brothers were involved!

Logic agreed with Jerry and Zeke. The smartest path, the path of least resistance was to tone the bar down and just play it straight. It was not up to Sid to change the world. It was ludicrous to even try. Business was going well, Sid's life was on course, and it was a course they could all rally behind.

Emotion had the toughest time with the whole situation. First with the Cardinal's attacks and now with the brothers. Turn tail and tone the bar down? Emotion steadfastly refused! The bar was a reflection of every self-doubt Sid had overcome since he was twelve, and the bar was better received than he ever dreamed. It shined with the purple aura of pride. Pride would not allow Emotion to back down. Not now, not ever!

This polarity clearly emphasized the shortcomings of the subconscious. Logic and Emotion exist to provide the poles of our psyche and limits on each end. They are port and starboard, black and white, yin and yang. They are seemingly always at odds, and, in many instances, a divided subconscious can be debilitating for an individual. It's up to a third party to balance the equation and lend stability yet tip the scale at the same time. For some people, religion was a guiding force in these situations. With Sid, Intuition was looked to in these instances, but had never stepped forward to fulfill this role since he had no idea how to do that. The new voice, overbearing and brash, filled this role immediately without even a splash of hesitation but three full fingers of sarcasm.

"The path of least resistance? Couldn't that also be Intuition's path of no response? 'Bend over backwards for the sake of brothers and the religious world in spite of the community Sid has created,' says Logic. Or 'Spite brothers and the world for the sake of acceptance and pride,' says Emotion. Let me say it clearly. This is not about Sid. It's not about brothers or anyone's feelings!"

"What to do then?" Logic asked.

"This little event changes nothing, so nothing changes. Irrelevance says stay the course," he said.

33

I met Sid right when the bar opened the next day.

"Did everything go okay last night?" he asked me.

"Funny, I was going to ask you the same thing."

"You worried about me too? There's a lot of that going around," he said. "I wandered around a bit after leaving, trying to avoid Zeke basically, but he waited up for me. He told me he talked to you the other day, told me. . . well, you know."

"Yeah? And?"

"I don't know. I mean, I understand his point. I can see why he feels that way, and I totally understand if he doesn't want to come in anymore, and I don't want him to not want to come anymore. I don't want anyone feeling excluded or offended, for that matter, but--"

"But isn't it inevitable?"

"How do you mean?"

"I mean, if you didn't want to offend anyone, wouldn't it end up just disgustingly generic?"

"Yes."

"The last thing you want is for it to end up like some bland chain restaurant!"

"True, but this isn't just anyone. He's my brother. It's a little more complicated than that."

"So, you should change because of him?"

"Maybe I should," he said.

"Isn't that what you did for all those years? Pretended to be someone for his and other people's sake?" He didn't speak so I continued. "And shouldn't he give a bit to meet you somewhere in the middle?"

"I know."

"I know it's none of my business, and I'm sorry. I didn't come here to add to your problems. I just want you to hear something then I will leave you alone."

"You'll leave me alone all day?" he asked with mock enthusiasm.

"At least until happy hour, smartass. Okay?"

"All right."

"You have to realize you are changing people's lives with this place."

"What are you talking about?"

"This is not just some bar, this is a safe haven for other Vegas Sids. It's an island unto itself, perfectly unique in so many ways."

"You're exaggerating."

"You built a new community here. A community unlike any other. You created hope for many people. You have changed people's lives. You have even changed me."

"I assure you, you have changed my life more than I changed yours."

"No, you are wrong. Did you know I no longer work at all?"

"I figured something was going on there, everything okay?"

"Everything is fine. I quit doing the consulting thing; I completely cut the umbilical and stopped working."

"Do you need some money?"

"Oh no. We are fine, Ellie's a professor, don't forget. There was no reason for me to continue to do it. I just couldn't let go until recently, and do you want to know why?"

"Why?"

"Because I wanted to spend more time here. I have to spend more time here."

"What?"

"It's true. This place is amazing. You are just having fun. I don't think even you see how certain people need this place. Imagine back to Barstow. Imagine if you, in that state of mind, walked into this bar. Can you imagine how much better you would have felt? Can you imagine how open you could be? How freely you could have expressed your thoughts, knowing, not hoping, that the people in the bar would not only understand, but empathize as well?"

"I hadn't thought of it that way."

"You are always working. I bet you miss a lot of what is going on."

"Like what?"

"A couple of Friday's ago I was sitting next to this kid who had just come in by himself and happened to sit next to me at the end of the bar. From what I gathered later, someone told him he had to check this place out, so he did. He just sat there, watching the goings on, listening to people's conversations, just like I do. Hank and his friend were arguing about what the stupidest commandment was."

"I remember that."

"Yeah."

"That's what prompted the tablets."

"Right. Anyway, Hank catches the kid laughing at something he said, and you know Hank, he loves it when people laugh at him so he drags the kid into the conversation. After a little bit, the kid says, 'We just buried my wife, and I can't help but feel all we did was feed the worms'."

"What? Really?"

"Yes, and if he says that anyplace else, it stops conversations. People would politely or impolitely ditch him and quickly too."

"Or worse."

"Exactly. That's my point. You can't say that anywhere except here. Heck, you can't even think it around most people."

"What did Hank say?"

"He laughed; they all laughed. Then, he asked the kid how she died. It turns out that they were high school sweethearts and had a spring wedding right before they were about to graduate from college. They were just married a few months when suddenly she dies from some kind of cancer."

"Geez."

"I know. Then Hank asks him 'are you sure she was dead?' The kid looks at him a little crazy and says 'pretty sure'. Then Hank says 'that's good, because how terrible would it be to be buried alive'. They spent the next two hours talking, and ranking, the worst ways to die."

"And the point of this story is--" said Sid.

"Nowhere else but here does that conversation even take place."

"And that's a good thing?"

"Of course," I said.

"Kidding."

"Oh. I know it's different, but we're different. You can't deny it. You tried, and it doesn't work. You react to things differently. You deal with emotions differently, but you don't fit in anywhere. That kid had spent the past two weeks listening to 'she's in a better place; she's with God; it was God's will.' He's had to smile and put up with. He doesn't believe it. He's sad, depressed, and it's only getting worse with all of the glum surrounding him, all of the mourners. He knows it's all irrelevant. He knows the pain of loss will only subside over time, and he just wants to get over it in his own way. He comes here, and he can laugh again. He can freely laugh and deal with the pain in his own way."

"Sometimes laughter is the only thing that helps."

"Most of the time. Actually, almost all of the time, but you need people to laugh with."

"That's true. So, I should just tell Zeke that although we may be a bunch of sick fucks, sick fucks need a family too and to deal with it?"

"Maybe not like that."

"Tell him that The Church of Irrelevance is here to stay."

"That works. The Church of Irrelevance?"

"I came up with it this morning."

"I like it."

"Me too. Listen, I appreciate the story, but--"

"I just didn't want you to think you were alone on this."

"I know but--"

"Lots of people need this freedom to escape the religious oppression they have to fake their way through everyday."

"I know, but I never really considered backing down. Thanks for arguing my side though. It makes it easier."

"Really?"

"I was feeling really guilty about it, but, like you said, I tried to live the other way, and it doesn't work. Nothing could make me give this place up. Nothing and no one."

34

When I arrived at the bar that evening for happy hour, the fire department had just finished putting out the fire. Sid was sitting on the sidewalk talking to a police officer with an oxygen tank by his side.

"Are you okay? What happened?"

"I'm okay. Everyone was able to get out in a hurry. It hit the wall by the prayer station. Luckily, it wasn't too crowded yet. No one was hurt. The fire went up the wall in a hurry and spread across the roof then the alcohol caught on fire. I couldn't stop it. I tried to put it out with the extinguisher, but I couldn't stop it," he said, feebly waving his hand at the decimated building.

"What happened?"

"They torched it. I guess it was two guys with masks and bikes. One guy threw a brick through the window, and then the next guy throws in a Molotov cocktail."

"Man. Any idea who?"

"I do, they left a calling card," he said and showed me a piece of cardboard with block letters.

COMMANDMENT #1: YOU SHALL HAVE NO GODS BEFORE ME.

COMMANDMENT #2: DO NOT USE THE LORDS NAME IN VAIN

"Shit. Cardinal Billy Joe?"

"That's what I'm thinking, but the officer doesn't think we have much to go on."

"What?"

"We have no good descriptions of the guys on the bikes. They don't think they will find any physical evidence in the fire. It will be our word against theirs on the threats. That's if we could even find them."

"That's bullshit."

"I know. Thank goodness you had me buy that insurance."

"What are you going to do now?"

"What do you mean?"

"Maybe Jerry and Zeke are right."

"No way. We can rebuild it."

"Are you sure?"

"Absolutely. Nothing has changed for me. Actually, it has. My resolve is now stronger."

"Good."

"Oh, and I had a great idea. We could build like an altar behind the bar, and keep all the alcohol on the alter. Like fake gold or something, what do you think?"

"I think that's awesome!"

"Yeah, me too. Definitely need some sprinklers too!"

This is when Zeke came running up.

"Oh my goodness. Are you okay?"

"I'm okay, Zeke."

"I just got the message, I ran all the way here," said Zeke.

"Everyone's okay. The bar's toast, but we can fix it."

"I knew it. I knew this would happen."

"I know," said Sid.

"People are so crazy, it was only a matter of time before someone did something crazy."

"Typical fucking oppression," I said. "Our way or the highway!"

"Hey," said Zeke.

"Al, it's not Zeke's fault."

"I know, I'm sorry," I said. "I'm just so fucking pissed!"

"Bulletproof glass," said Sid.

"What?" asked Zeke.

"I will put bullet proof glass over the front window so it won't happen again."

This is when Jerry arrived.

"Are you okay?"

"Everyone's fine," said Sid then told the quick story of what happened.

"He's going to rebuild it, Jerry," said Zeke.

"Why wouldn't I, Zeke?"

"Did you learn nothing from this?"

"Yes, I learned that I need bulletproof glass and a sprinkler system."

"Someone is going to kill you, Sid," pleaded Zeke.

"What do you want me to do, Zeke? Quit?"

"You could take the insurance money," said Jerry.

"And what, hide?"

"I don't know. I'm just saying that it'll be a lot of money--"

This is when the first media van arrived.

"Oh geez," said Sid.

"I was expecting that," said Jerry.

"I don't want to talk to them," said Sid.

"All right, let's get you out of here."

"Let's just go back to your place," said Jerry. "I will tell the cops where we will be and whatnot. Wait here for a second then let's get the hell out of here."

35

Irrelevance was the only one not surprised by the turn of the events. So few people understood their irrelevance and, as a result, most still behaved in a very human way. Fear is the most common emotional response when faced with an unknown, and many times fear begets violence.

A response would be demanded soon. A very public event had taken place, and the public likes to get into other people's business. Their idea had been ripped open, giving the rest of the world the opportunity to peek in. Questions were coming. It was time to rally the troops.

Still shocked by Irrelevance's appearance and subsequent tongue lashing, Logic and Emotion were completely unprepared for another bomb to be dropped in their laps.

Logic was wandering aimlessly around the subconscious talking about fire shutters and bulletproof glass, performing calculations of linear feet out loud and drawing something in the air with his finger.

Emotion, unable to communicate with anyone, sat on the floor in the corner insisting on going floating and soon! 'Immediately would work,' he said. 'Floating now, please,' he said. He repeated it again and once more for good measure. He wasn't going to stop.

Even though Irrelevance had done nothing but belittle and antagonize Logic, Emotion and Intuition since his arrival, by no means did he expect to replace them. It was only their air of self-importance that Irrelevance meant to attack and drive out of them with the sheer force of his sarcasm and contempt. Irrelevance too had a lot to learn. Fortunately, he could recognize that.

"Gang, gather around. Let's plan ahead here," said Irrelevance to get everyone's attention. "First of all, let me apologize to all of you for my overbearing behavior. It was not necessary. And I also want to congratulate Intuition for his tremendous reactions when the bombs hit. His response helped ensure no one got hurt in this unfortunate incident." This bought Irrelevance some much needed subconscious credibility.

"I've been very harsh on you, and I can see my approach was ill-suited for the end I hoped to reach. I've treated you as though you have no value, and that is wrong. I belittled and bullied you, and I will now stop. I attempted to pull you into the here and now rather than teach you about the here and now. That was my mistake, and I will work on rectifying it.

"Logic, Emotion, and Intuition have always been required to get through this world. One more than others in different given situation, but you are all equally necessary. All ideas and all perceptions have merit. They all contribute to understanding, and understanding should always be the goal, and understanding not just your perception and response, but also those of others around you without placing any one above the other."

"This unfortunate incident blew the top off our little secret. Lots of people will want to talk to Sid, strangers in the public and also those closest to him, so we must plan our response, who wants to start?"

36

We got Sid away from the bar without any trouble from the media, but it took less than an hour before someone called from the lobby of their building, the media had arrived. "No comment" was getting them nowhere, and soon there was a crowd of reporters waiting downstairs.

"Don't give in," I said. "If you don't want to talk, you don't have to."

"I don't understand what the big deal is," said Sid. "Why do they even want to talk to me?"

"Oh, shit," said Zeke from his bedroom. "Turn on channel six. They're interviewing Hank."

"So you think this was arson?" asked the unknown person sticking the microphone in Hank's face. The burnt shell of the bar stood in the background.

"Hell, yeah, it was. They threw a rock and a fire bomb through the window"

"You witnessed this?"

"No, Mike did."

"Who's Mike."

"Just a friend from the bar. He won't talk to you though."

"Why not?"

"He doesn't want to be on TV."

"Why would someone want to burn this bar down?"

"It's a centuries old tradition for people to destroy what they do not understand."

"Why this bar?"

"Because of the rally shots, the prayer station, and whatnot. Religious whackos won't go for that stuff."

"What kind of bar was this?"

"It's not just a bar. It's like my church. It's where I go when I seek enlightenment. We created these tablets out of grey whiteboard, I created actually--"

They cut him off and went back to the newsroom.

"I see," said Sid.

"They already have part of the story," I said.

"And they want to hear the rest from me."

"You don't have to talk to them," said Jerry.

"I know, but it'll be worse if I don't."

"Are you sure?" asked Zeke.

"No, but when is anyone sure of anything? It has to be done."

In minutes, we were downstairs to face the mob of reporters and cameras. Jerry forced them all to go outside away from the front entrance so residents could access their homes. He then had Sid stand on the side of a planter so everyone could see him better.

"One question at a time. Please keep it short. We don't care who you are. You can dub that in later. Just ask your question. We don't want to be here all night. Sid will start with a brief statement."

"Hi. I'm Sid. I own the bar that burned down off of Tenth Street. At about five o'clock, two men wearing dark ski masks rode up to the front of the bar on bicycles. One man threw a brick through the front window while the other threw a homemade firebomb into the bar. I was unable to put out the fire, but all patrons were able to get out unharmed. Questions?"

"Why would someone want to burn down your bar?"

Starting with the tough ones, as Captain Irrelevance had expected. Though Emotion really wanted a crack at this one, Irrelevance motioned for Logic to answer.

"Many people feel threatened by things or people that are different than they are."

"What made your bar different?'

Now it was Emotion's turn. "We pride ourselves in our tolerance of all people regardless of religion, race, or creed."

"What's a rally shot?"

Emotion carried on, "We are a Padre bar first and foremost, so, on occasion, patrons will do shots with the hope that the Pads score some runs."

"What about the cracker?"

Logic. "On occasion, patrons will chase their shot of tequila with a cracker."

"Why?"

Logic cut in just in time. "It's homage to the Franciscan Friars for whom the Padres are named. It's a ceremonial type thing." Logic is a much better liar than Emotion.

"Is there a sacrilegious slant to the bar?"

Logic continued, "No, and again, we tolerate everyone, religious and non-religious alike. Many patrons helped decorate the bar, so it was just a hodgepodge of different stuff."

"Who do you think burned down you bar?"

"I have no idea," Logic lied.

"Do you think the attack is religious in nature?"

"No." Irrelevance had to forcibly hold back Emotion while Logic answered.

"We met numerous people in front of the bar who were visibly upset over what happened. Do you have anything to say to them?"

Finally, it was Emotion's turn to answer, "Absolutely. We will be back and we will be better than ever! I will see you all real soon."

"I'm sorry. What is the name of the bar?"

"Currently, the bar doesn't have a name," Logic explained. "We have only been open for a few months. I wanted the bar to have a chance to name itself."

"I think that's enough," said Jerry as he stepped in front of Sid. "Thank you all for your time. We have nothing further to say."

"Who are you?"

"I'm his brother. If you have any other questions, you come to me."

37

When he was back in his apartment, Sid seemed relieved that that was over with, but he still had questions to face.

"Why didn't you tell them who did it?" asked Zeke.

"Yeah?" I said in agreement.

"What would that have accomplished?" said Sid. "The people that did this are long gone. We can't catch them. What's the point?"

"Justice!" I said.

"What is that? They were wrong. I know they were wrong. I'm sure they know they were wrong. Would bringing that out and making an even bigger fuss really have made us feel any better? Would it bring the bar back? The bar is gone. Nothing can change that besides rebuilding it."

"Expose the fucking hypocrites for the liars that they are!" I said.

"Even if we can't prosecute them, we could sue them and get damages," said Jerry.

"Eye for an eye?" said Sid.

"Well. . ." I didn't want to say yes.

"That is what you are saying, right?"

"Basically," said Zeke for me.

"Aren't we bigger than that? Isn't the goal to rise above all of that? To get past all of our human-ness and tolerate each other. Turn the other check?"

"But does anyone ever do that?" Jerry said.

"I am going to. You don't do stuff because it's what everyone does. You do it because it's right. To me, it's right because I understand what people are going through. People are going to see this as an attack on their beliefs. There is nothing I can do that will change that, but I'm not going to advertise that it may be attacking their beliefs. I'm not going to attack them for defending their beliefs. They have every right to do that. They have right to their beliefs no matter how wrong I think they are. Like I said, I'm not trying to change the world; I'm trying to survive it. Apparently, there are many people just like me also just trying to survive it."

"But people will take advantage of you if you don't strike back," I said.

"Only if I let them."

"How can you stop them?" asked Zeke.

"By being prepared for them. It was too easy for them to get me. Next time it won't be so easy."

"I can't believe you aren't more upset," said Jerry.

"Someone once told me to 'live in the moment; forget the past; forget the future; focus on right now.' Right now, I have a bar to rebuild."

"Who told you that?" asked Zeke.

"Al did. Right before I got on that karaoke stage."

"Oh great, and look how great that turned out!" said Zeke.

"Yeah, maybe I had it coming to me," said Sid, "but it's true. My every decision in life has led me to this point, right here, right now, and, even though I don't believe any of it was with a purpose, I'm still right here, right now. I can only change what happens next."

38

It took eight months to rebuild the bar. The fire damage was extensive, not just to the bar but also to the souvenir shop next door. Unfortunately, they did not have insurance and had to shut down, but that worked out great as Sid assumed their space and made the bar twice as big. Sid spent most of the insurance money on safety, putting in a new sprinkler system, bulletproof glass in the front windows, and a fireproof shutter he could close from inside that automatically covered the entire front of the bar. All of the interior construction we did ourselves along with help from many of our regulars. It made the project take longer, but the results were fantastic.

We received donations for the bar almost everyday of the reconstruction. Different people donated three TVs, five tables with chairs, and a dozen different bar stools which all created quite an eclectic collection of furniture. Someone also donated their shot glass collection, so now rally shots could be performed with shot glasses from around the world. Sid received so many pictures and paintings of Jesus, Buddha, saints, prophets, Padres' players, presidents, civil rights leaders and on and on that he had enough for three bars. But Sid thanked everyone and vowed to use them all, even rotating them if he had to. Hank made more whiteboard stone tablets, but this time he mounted it on actual stone tablets. Other religious artifacts, like crosses and figurines, Sid actually politely turned away. Publicly he said he was trying to avoid clutter, but maybe his hypocrisy knows some bounds.

The grand re-opening took place on Groundhog Day, February 2nd, Sid's favorite holiday. All of our old regulars were back and a whole bunch of new people came with them. Even at double the size, the place was still packed. Someone brought in a DVD of the Padres second consecutive World Series victory, and rally shots were flowing each and every inning! Jerry, Zeke, and I were helping Sid behind the bar, but we could barely keep up. Then, suddenly Zeke was gone.

"Where'd Zeke go?" I asked Jerry.

"He said he'd be right back," he answered.

"What's he doing?" asked Sid.

"I don't know," said Jerry.

"Shit. He can't take off. We need him," said Sid.

"He said he'd be back," said Jerry.

"You don't think it's the rally shot thing again, do you?" asked Sid.

"I hope not," said Jerry.

"I think we need more help," said Sid.

"Ya think?" said Jerry. "Personally, I'm sick of washing shot glasses. I do have a normal job you know, and it pays really well."

"This isn't a job," said Sid with his sly smile. "It's an adventure! You wouldn't trade this for the world."

"Actually, I would. I would trade anything to be on the other side of the bar!"

"Me too!" I shouted.

Suddenly, everyone was shushing and turning to face the front door. Zeke was back.

"What's he doing?" asked Sid.

"I think he's going to ask for volunteers to help us," said Jerry.

"Really?" said Sid.

"I have no idea," said Jerry with a laugh cut short by a wet towel hitting him in the face.

"Could I get everyone's attention please," said Zeke, standing just inside the door. "This is a very special day for my brother, Sid, and I just want to say a few words."

"Oh great," said Sid.

"Even better," chided Jerry.

"It took eight months of back breaking work to put this place back together, and doesn't it look great?" The crowd cheered. "There are countless people to thank, and I'm sure Sid has thanked each one, from those that chipped in to help rebuild the bar, to everyone that donated so many of the items you see in the bar, and everyone that gave us encouragement during the whole process. I think they all deserve a big round of applause!" The bar erupted in approval again.

"I have a few gifts I would like to present to Sid, gifts from Jerry and I as well as Al, one of the people most responsible for this place. Since Sid spent most of the insurance money fortifying this place, he couldn't afford to even replace his beloved jukebox, but what's a bar without a jukebox? So we are replacing it for him!"

Two strange men wheeled in a new jukebox to a roaring crowd.

"Quiet down. Quiet down. We're not done yet. Before we go any further, I have to admit something. When this place first burned down, I was sort of relieved." The crowd was silent. "A few of you know me as Sid's brother; a few of you know me as the cracker guy, but no one here knows me as a devout Catholic. I came up with the cracker chaser on a drunken whim and immediately regretted it. I saw this place as a symbol of my hypocrisy and as a danger to the safety of my brother, and I was relieved when it burned down. I admit that, but, now, I'm really glad it's back!" The crowd roared again.

"I was here most days after work to help during construction, and everyday I watched Sid interact with people who wanted to thank him, give him things in thanks, and give him time to help in thanks. Why was everyone so thankful? It's just a bar right?

"It took me time to realize that wasn't just a bar like I'd thought. It isn't just a bar to many of you, nor to Sid. It's a place unlike any other. It's a place that people go to seek shelter and comfort from the rigors of everyday life, to find peace and understanding and like minded people, to find community, and I realized that that's not a bar. That's much more. That's a church."

"And Sid is not just the owner or the bartender. He listens to people; he empathizes with people; he has created a place for all people to feel welcome, to express themselves no matter what they think, to openly mock worship, or to worship if so desired. People, this is a pretty unique place."

"Amen," I said.

"So a unique place like this deserves a unique sign."

"Shit, no signs," muttered Sid to no one in particular.

"Now, my brother doesn't want to put up a sign. He does not want anything that draws attention to this place. He figures people will find this place easily enough, and he only wants to attract the people that are searching, and rightfully so, maybe. It's been burnt down once, right?

"But I'm not afraid of it burning down again. This place is safer than the Popemobile, and I'm not afraid of attracting the wrong kind of people because experiencing a different perspective is good for just about everyone. Will some people be upset? Sure. Will some people react with anger and violence? Maybe. Hopefully not, but maybe, but that doesn't mean we should hide from it, right? Doesn't every church need a sign?" Zeke turned his attention to the door. "Hey guys, can you bring that in?"

They carried in a giant, four foot high, plain white, capital letter I. They put it down next to Zeke, who bent over quickly and to plug it in so it lit up.

"You weren't expecting a cross were you? Sid, what do you think?"

Sid was all smiles and gave him the thumbs up sign. Through his smile he asked, "So you guys knew about this?"

"No, I swear," said Jerry.

"Me neither," I said.

"What does the 'I' stand for?" Zeke continued. "It could stand for lots of things: information or ideas, because if you aren't learning you are slowly dying; ignorance, for another, something we should be conscious of and avoid--"

"Tolerate!" injected Sid.

"It could stand for 'individual' because every person is an island unto themselves and should be accepted as such, but mostly it stands for 'irrelevance.' Many eastern religions believe that only by destroying the self can you find true freedom. They teach you to recognize and avoid the sins of the self. Sid looks at it a bit differently. He knows that it's very difficult, if not impossible, to avoid sins of the self. You have to have fun right?"

"Instead of shutting out life, you can embrace life with one caveat, irrelevance. Irrelevance accomplishes the same thing. If your life is irrelevant, why worry about sins of the self? Why be mean? Why be angry? Why be selfish? Why hate, lie, or cheat? If you're irrelevant, these things are pointless. The past is just the past. You are just right here, right now, and nothing else matters, and as Sid said to us the night of the fire, 'you can only change what happens next.'

"But that's just an idea. A pretty great one, I think, but certainly not a required belief here. Here, you can believe whatever you want. That is what's great about this place. Everyone is free to believe what they want. As long as they tolerate what others believe as well, the Church of Irrelevance welcomes all!"

"Did you tell him about that?" Sid asked me quietly.

"No. You didn't?" He shook his head "No" as he watched Zeke.

"Oh, and everyone is free to drink what they want to drink!" Thinking the speech was over, crowd cheered loudly.

"Please, please, just one more gift. Last, but not least, his one is from me. As you know, the prayer station at the old bar was lost in the fire. It was the first artifact that gave this place its identity so I found another one. This one was actually from my church. They have agreed to donate to Sid. It has been sitting unused in the basement for years now after it was replaced with a bigger one, and I think this would be the perfect home for it."

They carried it in and set it along the wall where it used to be. It was twice the size of the old one. Zeke suddenly had a box of candles and began to put them in place.

"Man, I remember that from church," said Sid.

"Me too," said Jerry.

"Come on, guys," said Sid and led us around the bar to Zeke. He gave Zeke a big hug and thanked him.

"Thank you so much. You have no idea how much this means to me."

"I'm sure I do. You deserve it. Thanks for being you," said Zeke.

Sid then grabbed all three of us in a hug while the crowd chanted "Speech, speech, speech".

"This is awesome, honestly I'm speechless. Let's just drink, a round on the house!" The crowd cheered and stayed cheering, it was so loud you could barely hear the person next to you.

"Thanks for including us," I said to Zeke.

"Yeah, thanks, kid. You did an awesome job," said Jerry.

"No problem, guys. Oh. By the way, you each owe me thirteen hundred dollars, and my credit card bill is due in a couple weeks so the sooner the better."

Sid showed up with four shots.

"Here's to brothers and friends who are more than I deserve," said Sid.

"No. Here's to you, Sid," said Jerry.

"To Sid," said Zeke and I, and about half of the people standing around us. Soon everyone was doing a shot to Sid.

Afterward, the four of us just stood in the corner for a while just watching the raucous crowd. When the jukebox first played, everyone cheered. Every candle on the prayer station was aglow in under an hour, and many people stopped by to say they had prayed for the bar.

"Do you really think we're not going to have any more trouble?" Sid asked Zeke.

"Nothing we can't handle," said Zeke.

"Where did you come up with the Church of Irrelevance?" Sid asked Zeke.

"I saw you jot the note down on a piece of paper a long time ago, but I really didn't know what it meant. I understood what irrelevance meant to you on the night of the fire when I watched you talk to the media and wash away that ugly night so effortlessly and never lose the conviction. Then, when I helped build this place, and like I said, I watched you interact with people. It was just like being at a church function. Everyone pitching in and helping out in whatever way they could. That is when I understood the big picture. A church does not have to be about the worship part. It starts with the people."

"Just a sheet around the mattress," said Sid.

"What?" said Jerry.

"Just something Grandma told me in Barstow that day, it's all about people."

"Oh, yeah. By the way, Grandma is stopping by next time she's in town," said Zeke with a chuckle. "She can't wait to see this place."

"I heard Mom and Dad were going to stop by as well," said Jerry.

"Really?" asked an astonished Sid.

"Yeah," said Zeke.

"Man, I don't know about that," said Sid.

"It will be fine," said Zeke. "I can even see Grandma doing a rally shot!"

"We should franchise it," said Jerry quickly, like he had to get the idea out before it was gone. "As one establishment, you are a sitting duck for every crack pot and lunatic out there. If we franchised it, we could spread any inherent risk with many targets, and more gives the illusion of greater strength."

"That's a fantastic idea," I said.

"Go forth and spread the Word of Sid?" asked Zeke.

"Something like that," said Jerry.

"I've been thinking. People are leaving their stage of innocence, that stage of wonder and believing in fantastic ideas, childhood basically," I said, "but the next stage is puberty, growth, increased self-awareness, right?"

"Rebelling against authority and the beliefs of your parents," said Sid. "That's an interesting thought."

"What else do you think that will bring?" I asked to no one in particular.

"Oh, man," was all Zeke could muster.

"A lot of misdirected hostility," said Jerry.

"A lot of keeping to yourself or your small chosen group of friends," said Sid. "Factions, fear, experimentation."

"Yeah. Not good, huh?"

"I would say no," said Jerry. "Let's hope you're wrong about that."

"Yeah, let's hope so," I said.

As we stood there in silence, reveling in the Church of Irrelevance and all it had to offer, another song came on the jukebox and reminded me of something.

"Hey, have you guys ever heard of a band called They Might Be Giants?"

The End.

About the Author

Mike T Dark is a San Diego native and avid baseball fan. He lives in San Diego's North County with his young family. You can find him blogging about Padres baseball and Irrelevance at www.churchofirrelevance.com.

www.ingramcontent.com/pod-product-compliance
Lightning Source LLC
LaVergne TN
LVHW050638100826
845148LV00011B/1896

* 9 7 8 0 9 8 2 3 4 9 4 0 3 *